CW00566785

LOSING AT LOVE

a novel by
JENNIFER IACOPELLI

OUTER BANKS TENNIS ACADEMY,
BOOK 2

Copyright © 2015 Jennifer Iacopelli
All rights reserved.
ISBN: 0692369376
ISBN-13: 978-0692369371

For Grandma

Prologue

June 9th

La Metropolian Hotel
Paris, France

Indiana Gaffney gasped, her eyes flying open and locking on the glistening object across the hotel room. It reflected the muted television behind her, the French Open final, the red of the court, blurry in the polished silver. A large, round plate, innocuous to the untrained eye, with the sizeable laser carved logo of Roland Garros at the center, was braced against the mirror hanging on the hotel room wall. The mirror reflected the match clearly, the broad steps and fierce rallies of two men battling it out for the French Open Men's title. But those men were mere afterthoughts as her eye caught a set of shoulders stretching the material of his t-shirt thin, not a mere image from the television, but broad and warm and real. Strong hands slid down her back, fingers twining into the ends of her long blonde hair, tugging on it gently, drawing her gaze away from the mirror and back to the green eyes of the man in her bed.

He kissed her soundly, sending shivers down her spine and making her hips rock against his and her legs tighten around his waist. "It's not gonna disappear if you take your eyes off it," Jack Harrison muttered into the skin of her neck, nipping at it lightly with his teeth.

"Feels like it will," she whispered back, tilting her head to give him better access. Most of her mind was focused on what he was doing with his hands and mouth, but that plate, the one that declared in no uncertain terms that she was the new French Open junior champion, would not be ignored. Not even for the guy who made her heart pound like no one else ever had before, the guy who, up until a few days ago, could barely look at her without his shoulders slumping with guilt. Their age gap hadn't shrunk in the days full of soft kisses and nights far more intense — though perhaps not as intense as she'd like — but he wasn't fighting their attraction anymore. She hadn't chased him, not really, but he'd known she wanted him, almost from the moment they first met. Then he'd found out how old she was and he started treating her like a flashing red SEVENTEEN was stamped across her forehead, every year between them creating an accompanying foot of distance. In the end, the attraction had been too much, even for someone as painfully good as Jack Harrison.

"Hey, Champ, you in there?" Jack's voice brought her back, his lips spelling out the words against her shoulder.

"Champ?" Indy hummed and smiled. "I like the sound of that." In fact, she liked the sound of it so much she planned on winning again the next chance she got, on the grass courts at Wimbledon.

"I bet you do. Get used to it, baby," Jack said, his whole face lighting up as he shifted his weight forward, tilting her back onto the bed. A shriek bubbled up through her throat and the giggles followed as he leaned over her, bracing himself on his elbows and then smothering her laughter with the press of his mouth. As his tongue slid against hers, she turned herself over to it, letting herself revel in the dreams of future victories and the celebrations that would follow.

~

Randazzo Residence
Outerbanks, North Carolina

Jasmine Randazzo shifted her weight back and forth from one foot to the other, trying to appear interested in what the man in front of her was saying. He'd been talking about something to do with eligibility and options for the future, but Jasmine's eye was drawn by the large screen over his shoulder. As was tradition, her parents were throwing a party during a Grand Slam final. The next best thing to being courtside was to rub elbows with the US's tennis elite and make everyone feel like they weren't missing anything, when, in fact, they weren't watching the match at all. If they were sitting at Chatrier, they would all be silent during the points, heads whipping back and forth with the force of each groundstroke, nothing but the grunts and groans of the two men on the court echoing in the stadium.

"Do you understand what I'm trying to say, Jasmine?" the man asked, shifting into her view over his shoulder and trying to grab her eyes with his.

"Of course I do," she said, meeting his gaze for a second. "If you'll excuse me, I'd like to watch this last game."

Alex Russell was leading Henrique Romero of Brazil in the third set and was just a few points away from victory. Any other year, Jasmine wouldn't care at all that the best men's player in the world was about to win yet another Grand Slam, but this year was different. He'd spent the last few months training at OBX with them after coming back from a horrific knee injury. If he won, which all signs pointed to, that trophy would be displayed in the front entry of the training facility, letting everyone know exactly the kind of athletes that trained at OBX. It would bring an influx of talent, but it would also set a new standard of expectations. OBX wouldn't just be a training facility anymore. It would be the place you went if you wanted to be the best tennis player in the world.

Finding an unimpeded view of the screen, Jasmine focused on the court, a court she'd played on less than a week ago with her doubles partner, Indiana Gaffney. They'd faced the best doubles team in the world and after an embarrassing first set, they'd fought hard, made the final score respectable, and impressed a lot of people in the stands. Including, hopefully, the committee who'd issue wild card entries to the next Grand Slam, just a few weeks away now, in Wimbledon. That's what she had to focus on, not the other stuff, like losing in the second round of the French Open Girls Singles while Indy had won the entire damn tournament. And not the confusing mess that was her relationship with her best friend, Teddy Harrison. And definitely not that the man she'd tried so hard to ignore for the last few minutes was a college recruiter her parents had invited to the party specifically to talk to her about waiting until after college to turn pro and spend the next few years playing NCAA tennis.

The television was on mute so as not to disturb the conversations going on around her, but the closed captioning was on and a shot zoomed in on Alex Russell, tall, blond, and British, barely looking like he'd broken a sweat under the Paris sun. The black boxes and white lettering scrolled across the bottom of the screen: *Alex Russell, the man who everyone counted out just a few months ago, will serve for the championship and prove all of us wrong.*

"Come on, Alex," Jasmine muttered under her breath. People were counting her out too and one day, when she is standing on a court like that, just a game away from a championship, those people are going to eat their words.

~

Philipe Chatrier Court
Roland Garros
Paris, France

Penny Harrison reached down, her fingers skimming the top of the walking boot encasing her foot. The strength of the sun, combined with the body heat of nearly fifteen thousand people, was pressing down upon the court and a rivulet of sweat slipped down from the back of her knee, making her skin itch where the plastic rubbed against it.

Though she stayed seated, her ankle protesting against carrying any weight at all, the crowd around her was on its feet, applauding and shouting, letting their appreciation be known not only for the championship match but also for two weeks of tennis at its highest level played on the red clay baking under the new summer sun.

"S'il vous plaît, Mesdames et Messieurs. Merci." The chair umpire's voice boomed through the speakers, his words implicitly demanding and receiving silence or as close to silence as possible before such an important point. Everyone settled back into their seats, the cheers morphing into a buzz, electrifying the moment, the last one in Paris until next year.

Alex stood at the far end of the court, as far away from the player's box as he could be, trying to use the shadow cast by the court's walls for some relief. He was just a point away from another championship and proving to the world that he was back at the top of his game. Penny scratched at her irritated skin again, twisting her mouth into a frown. Maybe in a month that would be her, standing on the grass courts at Wimbledon, back from an injury and celebrating a championship at a Grand Slam. It would be the first in her career, compared with what had become routine for Alex.

"Come on, Alex," she whispered, knowing that even if he couldn't hear her, he'd feel her support across the court. Her fingers caught on the chain of her necklace, a large old-fashioned penny dangling from the end, Alex's good luck charm and his gift to her before the tournament. Now clutching it in her fist, she took a deep breath as he went out to serve the final point.

Alex bounced the ball beneath his racket onto the clay, a complete mess after three sets of hard-fought tennis, especially down at the baseline.

Romero was opposite him; bent over at the waist, shifting back and forth, ready to receive the serve. One last fan let his voice be heard, a deep British accent from somewhere in the crowd bellowing, "C'mon Russell!" A few anxious people shhh'd him, but Alex didn't even glance up. He coiled his body down, building power through his legs before tossing the ball high and, with a lightning fast stroke, attacking the bit of green fluff. He sent a low-lying laser beam across the court, skidding off the white T on the other side of the net and then past the outstretched racket of his opponent. The crowd erupted and Penny lost sight of him as everyone leapt to their feet, screaming, totally drowning out the umpire's call of, "Game. Set. Match." He came into view again as he was shaking Romero's hand at the net, then he looked up into the stands, his eyes finding her immediately. She blew him a kiss, but he smiled and shook his head. Jogging over to the stands and climbing in, passing rows and rows of people who patted him on the back before he reached her, covered in sweat and mud, he leaned over the wall surrounding the player's box and slid one hand into her hair, the other caught her hand and pulled her up against him, getting red clay all over her white eyelet dress as they embraced.

"I love you," she whispered against the whisker-roughened skin of his cheek.

It was the first time she'd said those words to him and they just slipped out. Panic shot through her for a moment before he pulled her closer, held her even tighter and said, "I love you too."

Chapter 1

June 14th

Outerbanks Tennis Academy, North Carolina

The rough terrycloth of her wristband soaked up the sweat at her brow as Indiana Gaffney swiped it across her forehead. Grass stains on her elbows, a gigantic bruise blooming on her knee, cheeks red from exertion; she turned to her doubles partner, Jasmine Randazzo, with a wild smile. The breeze off the ocean whipped over her, cooling her overheated skin as she raised her hand in the air and Jasmine clapped hers against it. Her chest rose and fell heavily as her lungs tried to pull in as much of the salty air as they could, the effort from that last rally catching up with her, but not nearly as bad as it used to, her conditioning finally at an acceptable level after her year away from the game. Of course, acceptable for most people was vastly different than acceptable for a professional tennis player, especially one coached by Dom Kingston.

"Nice one," Dom called from the sidelines, actually standing up and applauding with a broad smile slipping over his tanned features. But he then turned his attention to their training partners, two young men from OBX's Elite Boys squad standing flat-footed and winded, grumbling to each other in low tones. "And what the holy hell do you two think you're doing? Last I checked, this was the Outer Banks Tennis Academy. We train the best in the world. Did you think because they're girls they'd be easy pickings? Take two tours and then report back to the Junior Courts, I'm sick of the sight of you."

The young men trudged off the court still muttering and Dom's eyes narrowed. "Changed my mind. Three tours. Want to make it four?"

The taller boy nudged the smaller one with his elbow as they both shook their heads and said, "No, Coach."

"Good. Get lost."

They took off down the path at a measured jog, conserving their energy for the three laps of the entire facility, a circuitous route that would take them through the maze of forty-five practice courts, finishing up with a sprint across the sandy beach that lined OBX property.

Jasmine raised her eyebrows toward Indy, who smiled back. In her short time at OBX, she'd endured Dom's wrath enough to simply enjoy when someone else was his target.

"Ladies, that's enough for this morning. Cool down. Indy, get some ice on that knee before it blows up like a balloon," Dom said.

"It's fine," she said, glancing down at it. "I bruise easy."

"Fine, video analysis after lunch," he said before leaving them for his next training session.

Indy grabbed her water bottle and swished a mouthful before spitting it out. Too much water would weigh her down for the rest of the day, but she had to stay hydrated under the hot North Carolina sun as the weather shifted from a warm spring toward what promised to be a humid summer. Though, if she had her way, most of that summer would be spent a long way away from OBX, on courts around the world, starting with the grass lawns of Wimbledon. She swung her arms around in slow circles, letting those muscles slowly recover from the intense workout she'd just put in, before moving further down her body, twisting and bending at her core, then lunging and reaching for her legs.

"Better every day," Jasmine said, as they left the court headed in the direction of the locker room for a shower and a fresh set of clothes.

Indy nodded, pulling her long blonde hair free from its ponytail and running her hands through the sweaty locks. "I just wish they would make a decision."

"They" were the Lawn Tennis Association, or LTA, the English equivalent to the USTA and the people in charge of her fate for the next month or so. It was within their power to grant wildcard entries to the Championships at Wimbledon. After she and Jasmine pushed the number one doubles team in the world to a third-set tiebreaker, it made sense that they'd be granted a wildcard into the main doubles draw, but sometimes, sense had very little to do with what went on in professional tennis. They would both be headed there regardless, having earned entry to the Girl's Singles tournament, and they'd play doubles anyway, but after more than holding their own against the best in the world, playing doubles against juniors again felt like a total waste of time. Now it was just a waiting game and patience had never been one of Indy's virtues.

"It should happen soon, maybe tomorrow," Jasmine said as they entered the locker room; the buzz of dozens of girls echoing off the tile floors and metal lockers soon faded. Since their return from France, the atmosphere at OBX had been strange, to say the least. Indy was used to it. She'd been an outsider from the moment she arrived at the Outer Banks Tennis Academy, but her stomach twisted for Jasmine who'd spent her entire tennis career training inside the high fences of the best tennis school in the world. The other girl didn't know how to handle the silent glares and fervent whispers that followed them everywhere. Their partnership and burgeoning friendship was one of the hottest stories in the tennis world, but at OBX, where everyone wanted to make it to the top and most had the goods, it simply made them the targets of soul-crushing envy.

They walked side by side down the long hallway at the center of the room and made a quick left to their lockers. Indy tapped the second one in as she walked by. Penny's locker, empty while it's tenant was off in England recovering from her ankle injury and watching Alex Russell, the newly crowned French Open Champion, destroy the competition at Queens, the main prep tournament for Wimbledon.

"Have you talked to her?" Jasmine asked, nodding toward the locker while grabbing her shower kit from her own locker.

"Yeah," Indy said, wrinkling her nose. "She's pissed off that she can't train."

"Sucks," Jasmine said, before walking off to the shower room.

"Totally," Indy agreed. She'd never been hurt before, but just talking to Penny on the phone told her all she needed to know. She could hear the longing in her voice to get back on the court, to *do* something. Sitting on your ass while the people around you are working hard, getting better, as far as tennis is concerned, Indy couldn't imagine anything worse than that. Life, of course, that could bite you in the ass over and over again and Indy wasn't a stranger to that, not with her mom gone for nearly a year from cancer and her father—who barely noticed her existence most of the time—spending his nights with her agent, the high-powered Caroline Morneau.

~

The hot water was heaven after the morning workout. She took her time, letting her muscles recover as much as they could because she'd need them again during that afternoon's single's training. The locker room was blissfully empty as she emerged from the showers. Jasmine had headed to lunch with her parents, the facility's founders. She left her hair alone, knowing the warm air outside would make it curl, and pulled on a pair of white, terrycloth shorts, then a bronze t-shirt with the Nike swoosh blazoned across the chest in black. The shirt was a gift from Penny, who had more Nike merchandise than she knew what to do with after signing a lucrative sponsorship deal to become the face of their tennis line. Indy smiled to herself, knowing that one day soon, she'd have her own sponsorship deal. Caroline had said as much over and over again since they returned from France. She had made contact with all the big tennis outfitters and it was just a matter of waiting for the best deal and negotiating terms that brought in the most money for the most exposure.

Indy grabbed her bag from the locker, stuffed with textbooks and her laptop. There were just a few weeks between her and her high school diploma. Just a few more tests and she'd graduate in absentia from her former high school back in California, so instead of a nice, relaxing, mindless lunch, she'd be tackling her off-the-court nemesis, AP Calculus. It wasn't something she had to do as she'd easily qualify for a GED at this point. Her course load was completely made up of classes above and beyond the requirements for a high school diploma, but Indy was done quitting things. She'd given up tennis for a year and nearly lost her dream because of it. So she'd slog through calculus and all the rest and get that diploma even if the equations made her brain melt inside her skull.

Stepping into the sunshine, she shouldered her bag and turned toward the OBX library, running through the assignments she still had to complete, when a shadow crossed over her path, a large body falling into step with her, close, but not touching, their strides matching.

"Jack," she said, glancing up at him sideways, a small smile threatening at the corners of her mouth.

"Indiana," he said, echoing back her name, sending a shiver down her spine. He was the only one allowed to call her that, the only person who made the name she'd hated since forever sound friggin' good.

They walked together in silence, turning the corner that separated the courts from the residential area of the complex, but her stride was suddenly cut off when Jack shuffled his feet, sliding his arm around her waist and pulling her into a shady walkway between buildings. Her bag slid off her shoulder, but he caught it before it crashed to the ground and smashed her laptop to smithereens. He let it settle on the ground gently before leaning over her, forcing her to step back into the wall.

Walls were their thing. Their first kiss had been against a wall in a random hallway at Roland Garros, their second pressed against the wall of their hotel in Paris and now that they were back in North Carolina, they found any excuse to push each other against a wall and kiss until they were gasping for air and their bodies begged for relief. Jack's lips trailed from her temple, using the wall behind her as an anchor before bending his head to hers. Pushing up onto her toes, Indy met him halfway. She'd never been so grateful for every millimeter of her five feet ten inches as she was when she was kissing Jack. His hands slid through her hair, twisting it around his fingers, then cradling the back of her head, drawing her mouth more firmly against his. Indy brought her hands to his torso, gripping his t-shirt, letting her palms press against the cut of muscle that disappeared into his cargo shorts. The skin-on-skin contact made his breath hitch, his mouth opening just enough to allow her tongue to slide in, deepening the kiss, before letting her teeth nip at his bottom lip. A groan rumbled in his throat as he stumbled forward, pressing his body full length against hers. He wrenched his lips from hers, trailing his mouth over the line of her jaw to the spot just behind her ear. It was her turn to gasp and her head fell back as she arched into him. No one had ever kissed her there before. Jack smiled against her skin as her fingertips dug into his sides and she let a moan slip free as he focused his attention on that spot, scraping his teeth against it, then soothing that small pain with a flick of his tongue. Her hands scrambled to get purchase against his shoulders, desperate for some leverage, anything to help her slide her body against his. Then it was over, his hand gone from her hair, his mouth gone from her neck and his body inches then feet away. Indy blinked at him, trying to figure out why he pulled away when the voices echoing down the pathway toward them finally reached her ears.

Bending down, he lifted her bag as she ran her fingers through her hair, knowing he'd made an unholy mess of it. "You're fine," he muttered, handing her the bag and stepping further away from her as a group of junior boys stomped past them, none giving them a second glance.

"You have good ears," Indy said, biting her lip at the close call. If those boys had seen them, the news would have spread like wildfire through the OBX campus and everyone would have known by the end of the day. She was only seventeen for another few months, but that wasn't really the problem, seventeen or eighteen wouldn't matter to other people. She was a young tennis pro, he was an up-and-coming agent. The last thing either of their careers needed was the heightened publicity of a controversial relationship, even if Jack Harrison was far more of a gentleman than any guy she'd ever met. Sometimes, a little *too* much of a gentleman, truth be told.

Jack shrugged, glancing back over his shoulder again before facing her fully. "I'm sorry about this."

She reached out and took his hand, "We both agreed," she said, entwining their fingers, "it's just between us for now. It makes sense for both of us." Pressing his lips together in a thin line, he nodded, but she knew he wasn't entirely convinced. "Jack, we talked about this. You said you were okay with it."

"I just wish it were different," he said, tugging her closer, pressing a soft kiss to her forehead. His hands released hers and dropped to her hips, the edges of his thumbs brushing against her hipbones in slow circles, sending shivers over her skin.

"Me too." She wanted to scream it from the rooftops that this amazing guy was hers. That he had deep green eyes and a smile that brightened whenever he looked at her. That he was brilliant in ways that she couldn't even fathom with his degree from Harvard. That he'd fought their attraction for so long because of that ingrained sense of honor, like one of those heroes in a fairy tale, except Jack was real, flesh and blood.

"Have you thought...maybe we should tell Penny?" Indy asked, her fingertips landing on his forearms, gently stroking up to his elbows and back down to his wrists.

Jack let out a heavy breath. "Penny has a lot on her plate right now."

"I know. I just feel funny keeping it from her. Jasmine knows."

"We'll do whatever you want to do. This is your show, baby."

"I don't need a supportive..." she hesitated, almost using the word boyfriend, but that didn't really fit, did it? Not if they were keeping it a secret, "I need honest, Jack."

He leaned back, looking her in the eye. "Honest? Honestly, my sister doesn't do well with change. It freaks her out and right now, I'm not sure that the idea of you and me will go over that well. On the other hand, if we don't tell her and she finds out?"

"She'll be pissed."

"Yep."

"Maybe we should wait a little longer. We could tell her in London."

Jack nodded, "Face to face instead of over the phone."

"There's always Skype," she said, not really sure if she wanted to know what Penny, the only girl who'd made an effort to befriend her when she first arrived at OBX, would think if she found out she and Jack were together.

"There's that."

Indy shook her head. They should do it in person. They should have done it before they left Paris, but Penny had been so devastated by withdrawing from the tournament that it hadn't felt like the right time then either. "In London. We'll be there in less than a week. We'll tell her then."

"Okay, in London." They stood there for a moment, just breathing each other in until Jack leaned away. "I've gotta go. I have a meeting with a potential new client this afternoon and I've got to prep."

Indy snorted a laugh. "Right, like you don't already have a complete profile worked up along with potential sponsors to contact if they sign."

"You know me so well," he said, leaning around the building, checking the pathway for any more unwanted spectators. "I'll go this way."

Indy nodded back in the opposite direction. "And I'll go that way."

With a wink, he was gone, around the corner and out of sight, so she turned and adjusted her bag over her shoulder, heading out from between the buildings and toward the library. She'd have about half the time to get her Calc done than she originally planned. Fingertips pressing against that spot on her neck lightly recalling the feel of his mouth and the way her entire body was lit on fire by his touch, it was totally worth it.

"Are you sure that is a good idea?" a voice rang out from just a few steps behind her, the French accent giving its owner away, if the superiority and condescension weren't enough of a clue. Indy spun around and came face to face with her agent, tall, blonde, perfectly put together in a silk blouse and linen skirt, somehow looking completely cool and calm despite the blaze of the sun. She was in town before they all left for England, mostly to go over her plans for Indy's future off the court.

A denial formed on Indy's tongue, but she knew it was useless. Caroline had seen them and it probably just confirmed what she'd suspected for a while. Her agent was damn good at her job and it wasn't like she and Jack had been super careful about keeping private moments behind closed doors. "Good idea or not, it's none of your business."

Raising her eyes to the sky and shaking her head, Caroline said, "You are my business, Indiana."

"How many times do I have to say it? Don't call me that, and my *tennis* is your business," Indy corrected. "Keep your nose out of everything else."

"It is not that simple," Caroline insisted, her voice inching up in pitch.

"It really is." She turned on her toe and walked away, wanting to look back, hoping that Caroline's brow was furrowed and her hands were on her hips, lips pursed in aggravation. But looking back would ruin the moment because despite getting in the last word, Caroline now had the upper hand and it was only a matter of time before she used it to her advantage.

Chapter 2

June 14th

The student lunch crowd had emptied out of Deuce, OBX's restaurant, by the time Jasmine arrived, scanning the nearly empty tables for her parents, who'd asked her to join them for lunch. She'd been in such a hurry to get to training that morning she hadn't thought much about it, but now that she was walking into the restaurant it struck her just how weird it was that they'd asked her to meet them at Deuce when she could have just as easily walked across the beach and had lunch at home. Instead, they wanted the white table clothes, the stunning ocean views and the wait staff — witnesses.

As she rounded the corner, it all became clear. The man from the party the day of the French Open final, who'd been talking about the dozens of universities that would love to have her lead their teams to the NCAA Championships, was seated at the table. She caught her own reflection in the glass, an OBX t-shirt and jean shorts; her long, dark hair, nearly black thanks to her shower, was pulled up at the top of her head in a messy bun. Not exactly dressed for a business meeting, but if they were going to spring it on her, that wasn't her fault.

Her father and the man stood, politely waiting for her to sit down and join them. She did, plastering a smile across her face, the same smile she wore whenever she met any of her parents friends, the ones who expected her to be *something*. What that something was, she wasn't ever sure, but they expected it. That's what happens when you're the only child of two tennis greats; people *expect* things.

"Jasmine, you remember Felix Wolner from Elite Recruiting?" her dad said, smiling that same bright smile that he'd worn as he held up all five of his grand slam trophies.

"Of course, Mr. Wolner. Sorry, I didn't know you'd be joining us for lunch," Jasmine said, quirking a saccharine smile at her mom.

"It's Felix's last day in town and he mentioned that he never got a chance to finish speaking with you at the party," her mom said, with raised eyebrows and smiling that same sarcastic smile Jasmine still had plastered across her own face. She'd learned from the best.

She shrugged. "Well, it was a party to watch the final and since no one else was, I thought I'd catch the last bit of the match, just to keep up appearances."

"It was amazing, wasn't it?" Felix cut in. "Everyone had written Russell off as finished. Nice to see he had more tennis in him."

"Not so amazing," Jasmine said with a shrug. "He worked his ass off and he got results. It's simple."

"His physical gifts are tremendous though, you have to agree. Natural talent like that, plus hard work, that's what makes a great pro."

"Natural talent will only get you so far," Jasmine retorted. The conversation had ceased to be about Alex Russell, almost from the moment they'd started. "And all the talent in the world is worthless if you don't work at it." She took a sip of her water, trying to hide her smirk. This was too easy.

"Precisely," Felix said and Jasmine nearly choked on an ice cube.

"You agree?" she asked, setting her glass down and looking over at her parents. She hadn't expected that. At all.

"I do. It's usually a combination of talent and hard work that makes a great pro, that and timing," he said, eyeing her father, who nodded.

"Some players are ready as young at sixteen," he gestured to her mother, "others, seventeen or eighteen, and then others, perhaps not until they're twenty or so. Women tend to hit their physical peak a little earlier, but not all of them. More recently, with new training techniques, we're finding twenty or twenty-one to be the optimal age for a professional tennis player, though really, it's up to the individual."

Damn it. She'd walked right into that one. "So what are you saying?" she asked, tired of beating around the bush.

"Your parents asked me to talk to you, Jasmine, because this is what I do. I look at all the young tennis talent the world has to offer and I assess their abilities, figure out where they belong in the scheme of things so they have the best career they can."

"That's Dom's job," she countered.

"Dom's job is to *make* you into the best tennis player he can given your physical abilities. From what I can see from your recent play, in my professional opinion, he's done that and schools like Stanford, Harvard, Duke, they're all lining up to have you lead their teams for the next four years. And they'd like to give you a world-class education in return."

"And that's the best player I can be?" she threw up her hands and looked her dad in the eye. "That's what you're saying right? That right now the best player I can be is a college athlete? I disagree. I've been around tennis my entire life, Mr. Wolner. Indy and I just played against the best doubles team in the world, we forced them into a tiebreak and in a couple of weeks, I'm going to be playing at Wimbledon. Don't you guys get it? This is happening now. College is great for some people, but that's not what I want."

"Jasmine, mija, we're just trying to show you all the options," her mom said, reaching across the table for her hand, but Jasmine yanked it away, standing up.

"And this isn't an option for me and if you can't understand that, maybe you should stay out of it."

"Stay out of it?" her dad asked.

"Yes. I'm going to Wimbledon and it's going to be amazing and if you can't support that, if you can't get behind it, then maybe you should just stay here."

She didn't stay to watch her parents' reactions; she didn't even know if she meant the words that spilled out, so she just kept walking.

She made it to the video analysis room almost an hour early, determined to put everything that just happened out of her head. The only way to prove her parents wrong was to win in London. Indy would be holed up in the library with her calculus books so she had plenty of time to kill. Dom would insist they go over the day's training footage, but something about the way that the recruiter spoke about her recent performance was eating away at her. She'd played really well at the OBX Invitational up until the last set and at the French Open, she'd been at the top of her game during the doubles matches. The only thing that was left was how she'd done in the French Open Girls tournament; her first round match had gone fine, but that second round, that's when things went to hell. She'd been knocked out by a fellow American a couple of years younger than her, someone she'd never even heard of before named Natalie Grogan. Grogan played an old school serve and volley game, similar to Jasmine's own style of play and something you rarely saw anymore. She hadn't been prepared for it. If they met up on the court again, she was sure she'd do just fine.

She was just about to pull up the footage when Indy came flying through the door. "Hey, you're early."

Indy ran her hand through her hair, her long blonde curls spilling over one shoulder. "Yeah, I - uh - couldn't focus on math. It just doesn't make any sense at all, so I figured I'd come down here, see if you were ready."

Jasmine scoffed, unable to keep the grin off her face. "Please. You couldn't focus on math or did something *else* distract you?"

Indy collapsed into the chair next to her, bumping her shoulder roughly. "Shut up."

For a second, Jasmine considered telling Indy what happened at lunch, but her gut twisted at the idea. Indiana Gaffney's physical talents were the kind guys like Felix Wolner drooled over, but from a distance. There was no way she would waste four years of her prime at college, not when she could match her serve up against the best players in the world and come out on top. Indy would be nice about it, but she wouldn't understand, not really. So instead, Jasmine said, "You two have to stop being so obvious if you want to keep it secret. Not everyone who accidentally stumbles upon you two sucking each other's faces off is going to keep quiet about it. I'm just saying."

There were a lot of people who would love to have that kind of information on Indy, mostly the catty girls she'd put to shame the day she stepped on the OBX courts. Jasmine had been one of those girls and there was a time when stumbling upon Jack Harrison and Indiana Gaffney wrapped up in each other's arms, mouths fused together, would have had her making some phone calls to any media outlet that would listen. Now though, things were very different.

"I know," Indy said, trailing off. She opened her mouth to say something else, but then shook her head. "Let's just get this done, okay? If we can get it out of the way early, I can still get that stupid Calc done before my session with Dom."

"Right, that's what you want to get done," Jasmine said, tongue between her teeth.

"What do you want to get done?" Dom's voice carried from the back of the room.

"Nothing," they said together, glancing at each other before dissolving into giggles.

Dom strode in, shaking his head. "And to think, just a few weeks ago, you two nearly beat the living shit out of each other on the practice court. The good old days. Can you get yourselves under control long enough to analyze this footage or should I book another session tonight?"

Jasmine pressed her lips together and nodded. "Let's do this."

"Absolutely," Indy agreed, but as soon as Dom's back was to them to turn on the monitor, she dug her elbow into Jasmine's side, who promptly elbowed her back but then pulled paper and pens out of her bag so they could take notes.

"Okay ladies, let's take a look," their coach said, settling in beside them and starting the video. Their practice session today was relatively normal, facing two talented junior boys who could serve the ball hard and cover a lot of ground, but they hadn't proved too much of a challenge. Dom sped through most of the video, making small corrections on their decision-making: try a forehand rather than a slice backhand, don't hesitate on an overhead volley, mix in a few slice serves out and away. Plus a few physical mistakes, like Indy's tendency to overplay a volley at the net with too much wrist action or Jasmine getting too much out on her front foot on her backhand and her shoulder flying out before the ball had fully made contact with the racket, a problem she'd been working on for years, but had never quite figured out. She doodled BACKHANDS in big bold letters across her paper, coloring each letter in as Dom explained an issue with Indy's footwork at the net.

"All in all, not bad," Dom said, as the screen went black, "but it's not nearly enough intensity. Tomorrow, we'll start with Canadian doubles. You two against three of the guys. We'll start off with that as a challenge, but if it's still too easy, you'll be limited to the singles court. If you want to make it through qualifying at Wimbledon together and then fight through the main doubles draw, you're going to need it."

"Qualifying?" Jasmine's stomach sank.

Dom nodded. "Sorry ladies. Wildcards were announced about an hour ago. Looks like you're going to have to do it the old fashioned way and earn a spot. Indy, I'll see you later for your singles session, regular time. Jasmine, you want to start yours a bit early? This is Penny's usual training slot and 3,000 miles is a long way to fly for a practice session, especially in a walking boot."

Indy left them, grumbling about Calculus under her breath and they followed close behind.

~

"So I guess my parents told you about the meeting today," Jasmine said, as they matched strides toward her practice court.

"They mentioned they were bringing in a guy from a recruiting service. It's a decent option, Jas."

"It's not what I want. You told me a while back that not everyone can be a great player, not everyone was meant to be in the top ten, win grand slams. Do you still believe that's me?"

Dom stopped walking, considering the idea. "You tell anyone I said this, I'll deny it to my grave." She nodded. "I think that it doesn't matter what I think. Do your physical skills match up against the best in the world? No. They don't. You know that, Jasmine, but physical skills aren't always what wins matches. You've got to decide if you're willing to go through that, go into matches knowing that your opponents are better than you, knowing that if they play their best or even not quite their best, they'll still beat you. You've got to decide if you love it enough to play even though you're probably going to lose. Some players can handle that. Some can't. You have to be mentally stronger than nearly everyone else. You think Penny could handle that? Or Indy? Or Alex? Or your father? They couldn't, so you just have to be stronger than them. If you think you can handle that, if you think you can go out there and just play for the love of it, then tell the NCAA guy to take a fucking hike."

It sounded tough, so much tougher than training her body to the limit and putting her heart and soul into the game, because if she did that she'd have to surrender all the control to her opponent and the game itself. Could she handle that? Did she even want to? "And if I can't?" she asked, wondering if that was possible.

"Then college is a great option. Four years, maybe three depending upon how you progress physically. You'll be away from home, away from the kind of pressure that comes with being John and Lisa Randazzo's kid. College tennis is all about the team concept. It's fun and you'll get a great education, then maybe you'll have grown a little stronger physically, make the leap to the pros a little easier. Why don't you talk to Teddy about it? He made that choice a long time ago and you two have always been close."

Jasmine toed some of the dirt that had escaped the planters lining the practice courts, the orange and white flowers brightening up the concrete paved walkways. "We did, not that long ago. He said I should go to Duke with him." He said a lot of other things too, but Jasmine shook her head. Teddy Harrison wasn't important right now, at least not as anything more than her best friend. She'd let her feelings for him cloud her judgment more than once. She wasn't going to make that same mistake again. "At lunch today, the recruiter was talking about Stanford and maybe Harvard or one of the other Ivies."

"Are you really considering it?" Dom asked, arching an eyebrow. "Hard to turn down schools like those."

"I mean, I told him no, but I guess I have to think about it, don't I?"

Dom hesitated and wiped a hand over his face before he said, "You should consider it, Jasmine. I know you think it isn't what you want, but how do you know that unless you find out more? Explore it a little, give it a chance. It doesn't mean it's the right choice for you, just that it's a choice and it would be foolish to dismiss it out of hand."

She nodded, not sure what else to say. A warm hand landed on her shoulder and squeezed gently. Dom was rarely physically affectionate, so she gave him a small smile in return. "Thanks, Dom. I promise I'll think about it."

"Come on, let's get on the court. Whatever you decide, you still need to train."

"What are we working on today?" she asked.

"Full workout and then backhands, Jas. Backhands for the rest of your life. Whatever you decide, no coach in their right mind is going to let you get away with that crap you call a backhand."

She groaned, but a smile crept through. There was the Dom she'd known her whole life, barking orders and not letting good enough ever be good enough. "I'm going to start having nightmares about backhands soon."

"Good, maybe then you'll keep your shoulder in."

"Yeah, maybe."

Chapter 3

June 15th

Alex Russell's Townhouse
Egerton Crescent, Chelsea
London, England

Penny Harrison gripped the side of the mattress, tentatively pressing her foot against the soft area rug beneath the bed. A sharp pain immediately flew up her leg and made her entire body tense. "Damn it," she muttered to herself but felt the bed shift behind her. A warm hand slid up her bare back, tangling into the bottom of her hair.

"Alright, love?" Alex asked, voice still rough with sleep. The morning light was just barely creeping through the shades over the windows and the sound of people leaving their homes, car doors closing, engines rumbling down the street signaled the start of the day as well. The taupe walls made the room warm and cozy, despite the floor-to-ceiling windows, white molding outlining each one, and high ceilings, the same glossy white crown molding surrounding the room. The dark, nearly black, wood of his bed and furniture gave the room a distinctly masculine air. This was unmistakably his space, her luggage and some of her clothes strewn on the floor, the only feminine touches allowed.

She looked over her shoulder, blowing a lock of dark brown hair out of her eyes. He was leaning up on one elbow, dirty blond hair sticking up in all directions, the navy blue sheets pooling around his waist.

"Still hurts when I put pressure on it," she mumbled, leaning back into the bed and pulling the sheet around her as well.

"Doc said it would," Alex reminded her, his arm snaking around her waist, drawing her closer to him. "A couple more weeks at least, until you're at full strength."

"I know, I was just hoping…" she trailed off, then sighed. "I wanted to play in Birmingham and that's not going to happen."

The scruff lining his jaw rubbed against her shoulder, soothing in its roughness, before he kissed the skin gently. "Doc said that too. Grade two ankle sprain, four to six weeks, minimum."

"You never know, I could wake up one of these mornings and all the pain could be gone. Besides, he said it was between a grade one and grade two, the teeniest, tiniest tear."

"Very tiny," Alex agreed, sliding his fingers underneath the chain around her neck, pulling the old British penny from it's usual home against her skin. He rubbed his thumb over the metal, his eyes suddenly far away.

"It's not really Birmingham I'm worried about," she whispered, her hand resting over his, stopping the motion and drawing his eyes to hers.

"I know, love, I know."

Wimbledon was just a few weeks away. Her ankle might be just fine by then, but there was a good chance it wouldn't be and even if she healed up in that time, she'd have to miss weeks of training leading up to the tournament, the most important one of her life. After beating Zina Lutrova in the quarterfinals of the French Open, even with her ankle barely holding her weight by the end, the entire tennis world expected her to pick up right where she left off. She went into the French Open expected to do well, but she would be going into Wimbledon with everyone expecting her to win. The injury couldn't possibly have come at a worse time, right in the middle of the shortest break between Grand Slams. She'd been at the top of her game at Roland Garros, but instead, she had to watch someone else hoist the trophy from the stands with an air-cast on her foot, a constant reminder of exactly why she wasn't out there winning the whole damn tournament. For Penny, there was nothing closer to hell on Earth than watching someone else play while being told she couldn't. Even Alex's trophy, downstairs in his ridiculously gorgeous London townhouse mocked her every time she walked past it, though it would be worse back at home. Her parents would be fussing over her and she'd have to watch everyone else train day in and day out. She was better off here where she at least had London to explore and Alex to show her everything he loved about his hometown.

"Alright, no time for a lie in this morning, time to get up," he said, pulling away and grabbing his watch from the bedside table. "Paolo will be here soon and while I'm sure he'd appreciate how you look right now, he definitely doesn't want to see my naked arse."

The bed shifted behind her again and Alex groaned, his reflection in the window stretching his arms over his head. "You take the shower here, love, easier on that ankle," he said, gathering some clothes from his dresser and heading down the hall to another bathroom.

She hobbled over to where her suitcase was resting atop his dresser, digging through it and finding one of her dresses, only slightly wrinkled from the trip across the channel. They'd stayed a night in Paris, celebrating his victory at a nightclub with a name she couldn't pronounce and from there it had been a short trip to London. She planned on just calling The Dorchester, her chosen spot for the two weeks of Wimbledon, and starting her stay there earlier, but Alex had actually laughed at the idea and brought her straight home. It was a lovely house in a gorgeous neighborhood, all white town homes facing a small park with actual gardens in the back, a rarity in a city like London. It felt like something out of *Mary Poppins*.

The shower in the en suite was walk-in with a long bench that she could sit down on and keep the weight off her ankle and as the hot water sluiced over her body, she half wanted to call out for Alex to come join her but knew that was probably a bad idea. They'd get distracted, much the same way as they had over and over again the night of their arrival from Paris, when he'd promised his mother they'd go to her house for dinner and he'd forgotten about it completely. They had to start being able to reign in that desperate need for each other soon. It wasn't natural to want someone that much, was it? Penny bit her lip and laughed as she shampooed her hair. She decided that she didn't care. Natural or not, it was *amazing*.

Penny made her way slowly down the stairs toward the smell of coffee brewing and the sounds of a conversation, half in English, half in Italian, the words meshing together so seamlessly, like a completely new language. Paolo Macchia, one of Alex's best friends and his training partner while they were in London, must have arrived while she was in the shower. She felt her cheeks get warm, glad she hadn't given into the urge to call down the stairs and invite Alex back up to join her.

Paolo had been in Paris too, but she and Alex hadn't exactly been on speaking terms for most of their time in France, so she hadn't actually met the man yet. He wasn't playing at Queens and Alex probably shouldn't have either, but he felt a deep loyalty to the tournament hosted by the courts he'd grown up playing on as a junior. So despite being more than a little drained by the quick turnaround, he kept his commitment to the place that had given him so many opportunities over the years.

Smoothing down the skirt of her floral print sundress, she braced her weight on the end of the banister and leapt lightly off the last two stairs, landing on her good foot with ease. Leaning over just a bit onto her bad foot, the pain wasn't quite as intense as when she awoke, the hot water having done it some good.

Limping just a bit to keep her weight off of it, she stepped into the kitchen and let out a little shriek as she was immediately swept up into a hug, but not into the strong arms she was accustomed to. The man she assumed was Paolo spun her around and then put her down gently, before bussing both her cheeks with a kiss.

"Let me look at you." He held her back by her shoulders, looked her up and down, then nodded. "Perfetto."

Alex stood just a few feet away, leaning against the island at the center of his kitchen, a smirk playing across his face as Paolo finally released her. "I told you so," he said, standing up straight.

"Sei felice."

Alex nodded once, a serious expression on his face and suddenly it felt like this meeting was a lot more important than she initially realized. Penny twisted her mouth into a pout and raised her eyebrows, knowing they were talking about her but not having any idea what they were saying. "If you're going to stick around, you need to teach me some Italian," she said, moving toward the coffee machine to pour herself a cup.

Paolo nodded. "It's easy. I'll teach you."

"Where's your boot?" Alex cut in, frowning down at her bare feet.

Penny wrinkled her nose. She hated that damn boot. "In the library. I took it off last night when I was reading, then someone stole my book and decided to..." his hand slid over her mouth and muffled the rest of her words, his other arm sliding around her waist, pulling her back against his chest.

Paolo's face lit up in a huge smile, olive skin crinkling at the corners of his blue eyes as they twinkled in amusement, a lock of nearly black hair falling across his forehead, making him look even

younger than his twenty-four years. "I do not want
to know, but Alex, if we don't leave soon, they will
give our practice court away."

It wasn't true of course; they'd hold the
training court for hours for Alex if he asked them
to. Still, in the middle of a tournament where
courts were in high demand, being late and holding
everyone else up was considered bad form in the
pro ranks. Right on time, the doorbell rang,
signaling that the car scheduled to take them the
short distance to the courts had arrived.

"I'll see you later, right?" Alex asked as he
and Paolo grabbed their bags. His quarterfinal
match was scheduled for later that night.

She pushed up on her toes and he gripped
her elbow to help her balance as she pressed a soft
kiss to his lips. "I'll be there with bells on," she
said, rolling her eyes. As if she hadn't been at his
matches all week.

"Bells on?" Paolo asked as they both
shuffled out of the door.

"She's American," Alex said with a laugh
and Penny huffed in annoyance, but they were
already out the door and beyond her reach.

She limped into the library, a large room
with bookshelves stuffed to the gills. Alex always
had a couple of novels on his nightstand in his
house near OBX, but she still hadn't expected this
room to be quite so packed or the books so well
used. No one would believe her if she told them,
but Alex Russell, Britain's bad boy, was a closet

geek. She found her boot, right where she'd left it next to a brown leather sofa in the center of the room, and slid the stupid thing on, tightening the Velcro straps across the front. Now there was nothing but time to kill. Her phone was on the table beside the book Alex ripped from her hands the night before and, checking the time, she calculated the difference, knowing it was still the wee hours of the morning in North Carolina. That didn't stop her though as she ignored the night's worth of notifications, pulled up Indy's number and shot her a message.

It's 3am. Put the books away and go to bed! You have training in four hours!

She waited and then grinned when the reply came back.

Fuck you. Night! :-)

She tossed her phone down beside her, knowing Indy was probably crawling into bed. She picked up the book he'd given her, something about elves, by the same guy who wrote *Lord of the Rings*, but it just wasn't going to hold her attention. Tossing it aside, she grabbed the remote and switched on the TV, a flat screen monstrosity surrounded by shelves with even more books. Flicking through the channels, she found Sky Sports and settled in to watch a soccer match, a replay from the night before, but it might actually keep her attention on something other than the stupid boot on her foot.

"And Penny Harrison, basically on one foot, is going to try and serve out this match against the number one player in the world." The broadcaster's voice, filled with awe, echoed through the speakers. "We all knew how talented she was, heard everyone comparing her to Chrissy and Martina and Steffi, but this is something else, ladies and gentleman, this girl isn't just great, this girl has heart."

"Oh, no way. You've got to be kidding me," she muttered, as she watched a black and white version of herself limp across the beat up clay on Chatrier, the crowd noise fading quickly, replaced by the imported sound of a racing heartbeat, steadily slowing down as the camera zoomed in on her face, her pupils almost fully dilated, making her eyes look black. Her jaw clenched against the agony in her ankle, spiking up through her leg to the rest of her body, screaming at her to just stop and lie down, make it end. The sweat trickled down her forehead in tiny rivers as she tossed the ball up for the serve and then a black screen with the sound of her serve, her scream and then the crowd exploding, then silence as the Nike logo flashed broad and bold across the screen.

She grabbed her phone and flickered through her messages before finding one from Jack, who, when he wasn't being her older brother, moonlighted at her agent.

Nike is trying to capitalize on the injury. Commercial to air during Wimbledon. Call you tomorrow with the details.

Texting him not to bother, that she'd already seen it, she sighed, letting her head fall back onto the arm of the couch. Famous for winning, but not exactly the way she imagined. Gotta be more careful what she wished for as she just might get it. The only thing to do now was to replace that moment with a different one. Screw it. She was going to win Wimbledon, even if her fucking foot fell off in the process.

Chapter 4

June 15th

Indy loved grass. Not the kind of grass that the stoners used to smoke behind school back in California, but the beautiful, lush, green grass courts at the end of OBX's complex far away from the clay torture chambers she'd had to use leading up to the French Open. The frustrating effect that the clay courts had on her serve was reversed almost completely on the finely manicured lawns she'd be playing in England and it was a beautiful thing. Serve after serve, up the middle, out wide, into the body, it didn't matter, her serve was going to wreak havoc on each and every opponent she faced at Wimbledon and what her serve didn't handle, her forehand would. Grass even helped her net game, the surface allowing her feet to travel just a little faster rather than getting bogged down or sliding uncontrollably on the clay; she could keep her footing more easily and a dive for a ball didn't result in being covered in red gunk or feeling like she'd landed on solid concrete. It wasn't soft, but it definitely hurt less. She'd never had enough appreciation for grass before, but nowadays, it was her favorite thing in the whole world. Her game was made for it.

Her feet shuffled through the bright orange cones, pivoting on a dime, three crossover steps and then a spin, then a full out sprint to the baseline, leaning over it to shorten her time by another couple of seconds.

"Excellent, Indy," Dom called as she ran through the agility course. He turned his stopwatch toward her and she read the time, a smile breaking through the desperate pants for breath, her hands on her hips, sweat running in rivulets down her neck. Her entire shirt was soaked from the intensity of the workout but she'd cut even more time off her personal best. This is what she'd dreamed about before she came to OBX, working with Dom, feeling like every second she spent out on the court was one inch closer to being the best tennis player in the world.

"Walk it off, stretch it out and then grab some water."

"Let me go again," she said, swishing some water quickly, but moving to the start of the small maze of cones he'd set up at the end of her singles training session.

"You know who you sound like?" Dom asked, the question going unanswered. They both knew. She sounded like Penny and as far as Indy was concerned, it was pretty much the biggest compliment her coach could give her. "One more time."

She put her toe on the line, filled her lungs, exhaled slowly and on Dom's signal, she ran.

~

"Heard you have a meeting with Ms. Morneau this afternoon," Dom said as they gathered up the stray balls from the court.

"Yeah, she wants to go over some sponsorship stuff."

"She mentioned something about it. Just…" he trailed off.

"What?" she asked. It was rare that Dom spoke to her beyond what was going on with her game. She knew he shared a deeper connection with Penny and Jasmine after training them for so many years and it was something she wanted for herself too.

"I know I've said this before and I don't want to get in the middle, but be careful with how much freedom you give her, Indy. Tennis has to come first or all the stuff that comes with it, well, it won't be around all that long, if you know what I mean. I've seen people get caught up in it. Hell, I had to learn that lesson the hard way too. Just keep your eye on the prize."

"You don't have to worry about me, Dom. I know what's really important." She gestured around her to the court. "This is the only thing that matters."

"Okay, good." His eyes narrowed at her, like he was trying to see through her skin. Whatever he saw seemed to satisfy him, because he nodded and said, "Go on then, you're going to be late for your meeting."

"Crap, Caroline is going to go nuts."

Heading out from the locker room into OBX's main atrium, showered, dressed and running even later than she'd originally thought, Indy flew by the security desk, sending Roy, the facilities head of security, a quick wave. As usual, he was buried behind a newspaper, but still somehow managed to see her and raise his hand in greeting.

She found Caroline in one of OBX's conference rooms, usually used by the coaches for parent meetings and other official things that needed to be kept confidential. "Sorry I'm late, Dom and I ran over during my session."

Caroline's hair was pulled back in a neat twist, high collared sleeveless green silk shirt tucked smoothly into light gray linen pants. It was a stark contrast to Indy's cotton shorts and OBX t-shirt. Her agent tsked, letting her disapproval be known, but then simply gestured to the seat beside her at the long conference table, "Are you sure it was Dom who delayed you? Nothing else?"

Indy braced herself for the lecture she'd managed to cut short the day before when Caroline saw her with Jack. "Yes. It was Dom and if it hadn't been Dom, it's *still* none of your business."

"We'll see," Caroline arched a perfectly shaped eyebrow. Indy was about to protest again, but Caroline cut her off with a sharp shake of her head, "Let's get started then, since we are short on time."

Large stacks of paper encased in plastic covers, each with dozens of tiny fluorescent colored sticky-notes jutting out of the sides, were laid out on the shiny mahogany surface in front of an empty chair. Indy sat, staring at them for a moment before she said, "All these companies are interested in me?"

"There are several different piles. These are the companies that have expressed interest and contacted me with offers," Caroline said, motioning to the first pile. "Next, companies I reached out to and have made offers since. The last two are companies that will be interested perhaps after a few more victories and companies that have offered deals we should not concern ourselves with, though I felt it was, how you say, incumbent upon me as your representative to make you aware of such offerings."

Indy nodded, biting her tongue between her teeth, still not moving her eyes from the table. A soft laugh drew her attention away. She would have called it affectionate if she didn't know better. "Where do we start?"

Caroline tapped the pile closest to her. "We start here, with the bidding war I have facilitated for your outfitting deal."

The sides of her mouth twitched, trying to play it cool, but it wasn't possible to keep the grin down. "Bidding war?"

"Yes, mon cher, a bidding war. Though I must mention, the deals are not quite as lucrative as I had hoped."

Indy nodded. "Okay, why not?"

"It seems, after your most recent display in France, the usual sponsors are considering you and the Randazzo girl as a package deal. There is nothing in here that comes even close to the offers your friend Penelope was presented with after her junior win at Roland Garros. She and her brother did not jump at the first offer and it was very smart of them."

"So what your saying is the deal like the one Penny has isn't on this table right now?"

"Not while your partner remains an amateur. If perhaps you signed together, then while it would not be exactly the same, you would find it closer to the amount your talents are worth."

"And how much would that be?"

"Five million dollars annually for your main sponsor, be it Nike or Adidas or perhaps Fred Perry or Lacoste, though I think you would do better with a company that has a more solid foothold on American sporting wear. We should not discount the global market either."

"Right, okay," Indy agreed, her mind starting to spin, not really sure what Caroline meant. "So what does that mean?"

Caroline waved a hand at all the offers with a dismissive sniff. "For now, all of this means nothing. You must establish yourself more and then, we will see."

"Establish myself?"

"Yes," Caroline said. "Winning Wimbledon Juniors, that should do the trick."

"Well that's always been the plan, so you can let them know it shouldn't be a problem."

~

"There you are," she said, rounding the last of the library stacks and finding Jack tucked away at the table in the back corner surrounded by piles of paper, his laptop open on the desk off to the side. "Wow, that's a lot of stuff."

"Contracts," Jack muttered. "Penny's the favorite to win Wimbledon, bum ankle and all, and since the Nike commercial started airing, we've got about ten times the media requests we had before Paris."

"The commercial was awesome," Indy said, pulling a chair up beside him and dumping her bag on the table. "Mind some company?"

"Have a seat. Calculus?"

"How'd you guess?"

"Wild stab in the dark. How'd the meeting go with the She-Devil?"

Indy flinched. "The meeting was fine, but…" she trailed off.

"But…" he echoed.

Better to just rip the friggin' Band-Aid off. "She knows about us," she said quickly, her words blending together, but one look at his face and she knew he understood. He made the same face as his little sister when she was unhappy about something, his lips forming a thin line, green eyes narrowing, not in anger, but in annoyance.

"Caroline's sharp; I'm actually surprised she didn't figure it out sooner." He rubbed at his face, sitting back in his chair. "What did she advise you?"

Indy's brow furrowed as she leaned forward, elbows on her knees, a hand landing upon his thigh. "I told her it wasn't any of her business."

Jack took her hand in his, entwining his fingers with hers. "Baby, it is her business. She's your agent, it's her job to protect you in situations like this."

"Situations like what?"

"Situations that are potentially damaging to your reputation as a professional."

"You're not a situation, Jack," she said, not liking this conversation at all.

"You know what I mean."

She could see him pulling away, not actually, but in his eyes, the set of his shoulders, the sudden tension in his hand. She made a choice. She raised their joined hands to her lips, pressing a kiss against his wrist before sliding out of her chair, but not rising, simply slipping into his lap. "Pretty sure I can't sit in a situation's lap," she whispered, settling his hand against her hip before taking his face in her hands, brushing her thumb across his mouth. His tongue snuck out, nudging her finger and she smiled before leaning in and catching his lower lip between hers, nipping at it lightly.

One of his hands slid around to the small of her back, drawing her body tightly against his; the other hand cupped the back of her head, fingers twisting into her hair, tugging on it just a little and then harder as she groaned into his mouth and arched into him. Whenever they were together, Indy felt like he was always testing, figuring out what she liked and giving her a little more of it every time. It was how he approached everything, that brilliant mind of his experimenting until he found just the right formula for success. Just as the thought crossed her mind, he wrenched his mouth away from hers. Then, with the slightest increase in pressure from his thumb, he angled her head just right, his lips finding that spot just below her ear that he'd discovered the day before, closing around it in a hot, wet kiss. Her entire body jumped at the contact.

"Fuck." The word slipped out, but it seemed to spur him on. He stood quickly, settling her on the table. Indy's hands fumbled at his shoulders, trying to find purchase there and keep their bodies close, but he didn't let her get far, his hands at her hips, flexing against them for a moment before pulling her against him, groans escaping their throats in harmony.

"Do you know what you do to me, baby?" he asked, but she responded without words, shifting her hips, feeling his reaction to her. "Shit," he ground out from between clenched teeth. "We can't...Indiana; we can't do this here."

She leaned back, trying to catch her breath, but it was nearly impossible with his mouth still hovering over her pulse point.

"Okay," she said, trying to untangle herself from him, but only succeeding in rubbing full length against him.

"Fuck, Indiana," he said, his head dropping to her shoulder.

"Sorry," she said, her tone letting him know she wasn't sorry at all.

"Yeah, you sound it." Finally he stepped away from her, giving her the space to climb down off the table. He fell into his chair and she sat back down on hers and the moments bled together as they simply sat in silence. No awkwardness, just a comfortable quiet.

"It's getting harder to stop," she said, her voice still laced with everything she felt for him.

Jack chuckled, "It's always been hard to stop."

"You have it down to an art form."

"Yeah well, what I have in mind is not going to happen on a library table where anyone could walk in on us."

Indy bit her lip. There was a note in his voice she'd never heard before. "What do you have in mind?"

He lifted an eyebrow. "Indiana, when we're together for the first time, it's not going to be some quickie with my pants around my ankles and your shorts on the floor. I know exactly what you need, baby, and once we have a little bit of privacy, I'm going to take my time giving it to you."

She swallowed before taking her lip between her teeth, biting down hard. Jack smirked and she could practically see him filing away her reaction in his mind, knowing she liked it when he talked to her like that.

"I, um, I have…" she cleared her throat and ran a hand through her hair, unable to look away from him.

"Calculus?" he asked, tapping the book on the table that they'd managed to avoid sending to the floor with most of Jack's paperwork.

Indy nodded, feeling her heart rate struggling to even out. "Calculus," she agreed, opening the book with a shaky hand and trying to remember the page number of her assignment.

"Hey," Jack said, covering her hand with his. The fire in his eyes wasn't gone, but it was down to embers compared with the raging inferno just moments before. "You want some help?"

With a final, heavy breath, she smiled. "Yeah, you any good at vector functions?"

"I happen to be excellent at vector functions."

"A man of many talents," she said, her eyes twinkling at him.

"Don't start that again," he said, waving his hand at the book. "You've got functions to graph."

Chapter 5

June 17th

Jasmine unplugged her phone from its charger and tucked it into her racket bag. She glanced around her bedroom to make sure she wasn't forgetting anything, then lifted the strap over her head, across her body. She turned and her heart skipped a beat when she saw her father leaning against the arch of her doorway, mug of coffee in his hand.

"Off to practice?" he asked, though the answer was obvious.

Jasmine nodded. "I should go. I'll be late."

"Teddy won't mind."

She just shrugged and looked away, pretending the pile of laundry in the corner was fascinating.

"Did you mean what you said? You don't want us to come to London?"

"I want you there, but not if you can't support me."

He stood tall, his shoulders straightening, his voice rising in volume. "Of course we support you."

"You don't support what I want. You don't support *my dream* and I don't need a reminder of that every time I see you guys from the court. Now I really am going to be late."

She pushed past him, her shoulder colliding with the side of the doorway as her dad stood there, stunned at her words. He didn't bother calling her back and she flew down the stairs, out the backdoor and sprinted across the beach to OBX.

She leaned against the fence of the grass practice courts, trying to catch her breath, staring out onto the water as the sun rose over the beach. A perfect moment, the kind you see in movie montages where the athletes are training hard for the upcoming tournament, the big game, scene after scene of wiping sweaty foreheads, taking long sips from water bottles before putting them down and starting again. If only it were like that. If only you could have a training montage and just *be better*. In real life, you had to work for it, you had to feel every agonizing millisecond of every single training session and even then, sometimes, no matter how hard you pushed, none of it mattered and you had to push out the voices of your parents and coaches and friends who have lower expectations for you than you have for yourself. You just have to do it.

The chain link fence shifted behind her and a shoulder bumped into hers. "Hey," Teddy Harrison said, crossing his arms over his chest. "Nice view."

"Same as always," she said with a shrug. "You ready?"

"To kick your ass? Damn straight I am."

They stretched out together, warmed up and fell into their old routine even though they hadn't met up in the morning like this in a long time, not since before Indy had arrived at OBX. Teddy's commitment to tennis began and ended with the fact that he happened to be good at it and that it was going to pay for four years at Duke. As soon as he'd given a verbal commitment to the school in the fall of his junior year, his dedication to rising before the sun and meeting her on an empty practice court had waned and so she compromised, moving their sessions to later in the day to allow him to sleep in. Compromise, at least on her end, had pretty much defined their relationship for the last couple of years, right until the moment they'd drunkenly pressed their mouths and less innocent parts of their bodies together a few months ago. Everything had changed that day and they fumbled to try and sort out their friendship. But things were better now and that was the important thing. Even if he didn't feel about her the way she felt about him, anything was better than losing him completely. At least, that's what she was able to tell herself while he was three thousand miles away.

"What do you want to work on today?" he asked, rotating his left arm in large circles.

"Nothing. I just want to play. Let's just play, okay?"

He flashed her a thousand-watt smile and her stomach tightened, but she fought the reaction. "Alright then, it's on. You serve," he said, tossing her a ball.

Jasmine flounced to the baseline. If he was going to be stupid enough to give her the advantage right off the bat, who was she to complain? A few bounces of the ball at her feet, then coiling down, letting her body explode up and through the ball, sending a well-placed serve up and out to his weaker, backhand side immediately. He returned it well enough and Jasmine saw him smile as his return mimicked her serve, forcing her to the backhand as well. It was the look of someone who knew his opponent's weakness.

Jasmine crossed over, compelling her shoulder to stay in and fired a backhand up the line and out of his reach for a winner. "15-Love," she said, not even bothering to check for the shock on his face, instead pulling a ball from the hidden pocket inside the leg of her shorts and striding back to the service line.

By the time she looked up, ready to start the next point, he'd obviously gotten over it, and was bent over waiting for her to serve. He twisted the racket in his hands once, then twice. It was one of his tells. She'd pissed him off with that winner and played right into her hands.

Her next serve was straight up the white T in the center of the court and Teddy, letting his aggravation get the best of him, anticipated the serve, stepped around it and fired a forehand ten feet beyond the baseline.

"30 – Love," she sang out as he retrieved the ball and tossed it back over to her side of the net.

"Don't get cocky," he shot back, twirling his racket again.

She piggybacked the serve up the T, then went charging up to the net, finally playing to her own strength, intercepting his return and spinning a short volley. It bounced twice, long before he could reach it.

A voice, familiar but completely unexpected, rang out from the sidelines. "Three in a row, Harrison. Maybe you should forfeit."

Springy black curls and cocoa skin, a bright red t-shirt with a bold white Stanford across the chest, Amy Fitzpatrick, a girl who hadn't set foot on OBX grounds for two years, was standing at the gate to their court, a huge smile on her face, looking just as gorgeous as the day she left for college and broke Teddy's heart.

Jasmine felt her racket slip through her fingers, landing on the grass court with a soft *thump*. "Amy. Oh my God, what are you..." she trailed off.

"Dom invited me down to work with the summer camps once school let out and I couldn't say no. As soon as I got here, I asked Roy where you were. Not surprised to find you here, Jazzy, but Teddy Harrison out of bed at this hour? That's like some kind of miracle. The Teddy I remember liked to stay in bed as much as he could."

Two years at Stanford hadn't done much for Amy's subtlety.

"Amy," Teddy grunted out. Jasmine flickered her gaze toward him, already knowing what she'd see. His jaw was clenched, the veins in his neck standing out and his shoulders were held up high and tense.

"Two years and that's all I get?" Amy asked, finally stepping through the gate and moving onto the court. Not giving Teddy a chance to move away before she wrapped her arms around his shoulders and pressed her lips to the corner of his mouth. Teddy stiffened and put his hands on her hips, moving her body away from his gently. The corner of her mouth quirked up as she looked Teddy up and down. "You look good, Harrison."

A harsh rasp escaped from Teddy's throat. "Thanks, Amy, you too." He looked to Jasmine and she opened her mouth to say something, but no words came out.

"And Jazzy. Look at you, exactly the same as I left you! Come here!" A split second later, it was Jasmine wrapped up in the arms of her former best friend, the girl who'd dumped Teddy before she left, but simply faded from Jasmine's life after a week or so away at school. The loss of friendship hurt Jasmine, especially since Amy hadn't had the decency to at least *try* and keep in contact, but she'd gotten over it when the other OBX girls started to look up to her the way she had looked up to Amy. Teddy, on the other hand, had been completely devastated and had never settled into a relationship since, keeping things casual with as many girls as would have him.

"I'll um, I'll just leave you guys to it then," Teddy said, rubbing the back of his neck.

Amy pulled away from Jasmine and reached out for him, grabbing his wrist. "No, you two were in the middle of a session. Don't let me interfere."

"Nah, you two have catching up to do, I'm sure. I'll just, I'll see you later, Jas," he said, but before he left, he leaned down and kissed her, his lips brushing the corner of her mouth, almost exactly as Amy had kissed him. Jasmine flinched back and blinked at him, but he was already walking off the court, twirling the racket in his hand over and over again.

Amy watched him go as well but then turned to Jasmine with her eyebrows raised. "If I had known that skinny kid I dumped was going to turn into *that* fine specimen, I might not have let him go so easily."

Jasmine swallowed down the nasty retort that bubbled up from her chest and shook her head. "I'm glad you got here before we left for London. It'll be nice to catch up."

"London?"

"Yeah, um, Wimbledon? I'm playing juniors and I'm in the qualifying for women's doubles."

Letting out a little laugh, like somehow, that wasn't a big deal, Amy said, "Oh right. It's perfect timing. I can't believe Dom made you play doubles with that girl. Like what did he think, it was going to make up for him letting her train here and stealing your title?"

Jasmine felt her shoulders grow heavy, every reason why she hadn't really mourned the end of her friendship with Amy suddenly weighed her down.

"And what was that with Teddy just now? You two are like together now or something?"

"No. We're just friends. I don't know what that was."

"But you liked him for so long, even when I was dating him. "

"Before," Jasmine said, softly. "I liked him *before* you started dating him."

"Oh that's right. We both had a thing for him back then. That was so funny. Good for you though. I mean you and Teddy. That's *such* a bad idea. Let's go to Deuce, I want to hear about *everything*."

As they walked through the academy's grounds, people stopped to wave and say hello to Amy at nearly every turn. She'd been one of the first students to come and train at OBX and one of its early success stories. Signing a NLI to Stanford and becoming an All American as a freshman, she had helped Stanford to a NCAA Championship.

"Oh wow, is that her?" Amy asked, drawing to a complete stop just off to the side of one of the half courts where Indy was hitting against the wall, feet flying over the hard court. "She should like model or something, go all Anna Kournikova instead of wasting her time on the court."

"She's good, really good."

"Penny good?" Amy asked, practically spitting out the other girl's name.

Jasmine chose her words carefully. She knew how Amy worked and she didn't need rumors swirling around OBX that she'd said Indy's game sucked. "Different. Less refined, more powerful."

"I heard she had a serve on her."

"It's incredible," Jasmine said and then decided to get a little dig in of her own. "Didn't you see us in France? We were on ESPN."

Amy waved her hand dismissively and shrugged. "A little bit, but not much. I was really busy."

"Right, of course," Jasmine said, knowing she'd hit her mark. "Come on. Let's go grab some lunch."

"Jas!" Indy called and Jasmine groaned. She was hoping to put this off for a little longer. The tall blonde jogged over to the fence and grabbed a sip from her water bottle.

"Hi there," Amy said. "Amy Fitzpatrick."

"Indi-"

"Indiana Gaffney, I know." Indy tilted her head and raised an eyebrow at Jasmine and smirked.

"Amy used to train here and now she's at Stanford," Jasmine said, feeling the air swirling with tension around them, growing thicker by the second.

"Nice to meet you."

"You too. Jazzy and I were just going to get lunch. You should so come with us."

Indy's smirk grew. "Thanks, but I've gotta finish up here and then I promised Penny a Skype call."

"That's right. She's over in London, isn't she?" Amy asked with a significant look at Jasmine. "Penny the Ice Princess and Alex Russell, who would have guessed that?"

"Ice Princess?"

Amy laughed. "Yeah, she barely let anyone near her for years around here let alone a guy."

"Right, okay," Indy said. "I'll see you guys later I guess. I gotta get this done."

They were just a few steps away from the fence when Amy laughed and laced her arm through Jasmine's. "Wow, what a total bitch. So fake."

Jasmine rolled her eyes and pulled away. Indy was one of the most genuine people she'd ever met. What you saw was what you got, good or bad.

"You know what Amy, I think I'm going to have to take a rain check on lunch."

Amy stopped dead in her tracks and stuck her lower lip out. "You're kidding? Come on, we haven't seen each other in forever."

"I just remembered, I have a meeting with…" she trailed off, stalling for time when just over Amy's shoulder Jack Harrison stepped into her view. "Jack Harrison. I have a meeting with Jack."

"Jack Harrison?" Amy asked, following the line of Jasmine's eyes.

"Hi, sorry, do I know you?" Jack asked, politely turning toward her. As far as Jasmine knew, they'd never met before. He'd been away at school when Amy and Teddy dated, but Jack was a pretty recognizable face in tennis nowadays.

"Jack, this is Amy…*Amy Fitzpatrick.*" Immediately his usually open and friendly features darkened. He might not *know* Amy, but he definitely knew *of* her. "I was just telling her that I had a meeting with you so we couldn't have lunch."

Jack caught on quickly, not even letting his understanding pass over his face. "I was just coming to look for you."

"Sorry, Amy, maybe some other time, okay?"

Her lips were pursed as she looked back and forth between them and shrugged, a smile suddenly overtaking her features, but not reaching her eyes. "No problem at all. I guess I'll just see you later, Jazzy."

She walked away toward the main atrium and Jasmine let out a heavy breath. "Cross Stanford off my list," she muttered and then turned back to Jack. "Thanks for that, by the way."

"Always happy to be of service," he said with a grin. "So that was the girl who had my baby brother all tied up in knots?"

"That was her. She found me and Teddy on the grass courts practicing. He…he sort of ran away."

Jack nodded. "What he does best."

"You don't have to tell me that." The words slipped out before she even had time to fully think them. "Um, I mean…"

"Yeah, you'd know that better than anyone, I guess," Jack said, reaching out and giving her shoulder a squeeze. "I'm gonna go find him, unless you actually need to meet with me about something?"

"Actually, I was wondering," she trailed off. "If you want to, it's totally cool if you say no, but my parents hired this recruiter, Felix —"

"Wolner. Yeah, I know him," Jack said, cutting her off.

"He mentioned something about Harvard and if you had the time…"

"You're thinking about Harvard?"

"I'm weighing my options," she said, the words becoming true as she said them. It wasn't like what her parents and Felix and Dom had said didn't make sense, but if she was going to make a choice like this, she wanted it to be *her* choice and not theirs. "And if you can keep that between us, I'd really appreciate it."

"Of course. That's nobody's business except yours. And if you want to talk about Harvard, Jasmine, then you've come to the right place."

~

They wandered back toward where Indy was hitting, Jack rambling about the amazing experience he had in Cambridge. Three years of tennis, great friendships, the best professors in the world. Even being away from his family, something he thought was going to be rough, actually turned out to be really good for him.

"That sounds great," she said and he arched an eyebrow at her. "Not that I don't love my parents and all, but…"

"Can't be easy being their kid around here," Jack finished for her.

"Exactly."

A bubbly sort of tune rang up from the general vicinity of his shorts pocket as they finally made it back to where Indy was still training, having moved on to backhands.

Jack checked the screen. "It's Penny. I gotta take this."

"Sure," she said, leaning her elbows on the fence and watching Indy finish up a set.

"So, who was that exactly?" Indy asked, as she let the last ball fly past her and bounce into the fence.

"My best friend," Jasmine said. "Former best friend. Your boyfriend rescued me. She's not exactly his favorite person."

"Oh, is she the one…. Jack told me a while back about what she did to Teddy."

"Yeah, she pretty much destroyed him for any other girl who came after," she said, remembering the press of Teddy's lips against hers just a few minutes before, the tension in his entire body. The sooner they all left for London, the better.

"He's got to grow up and get over it eventually though. Wasn't it like two years ago? Maybe her being back'll be the push he needs toward you, you know…"

"What?"

"Shit or get off the pot."

"Ugh, Indy, really?"

"Well, I'm just saying. You two make sense in all the ways that matter and he's just being ridiculous."

"Whatever. Change of subject please. We've beaten this to death, haven't we?"

"Fine. What were you and Jack talking about?"

"He was telling me about Harvard."

Indy laughed. "He could talk about that for days if you let him."

"You were going to go there, weren't you?"

"I was thinking about it. My dad went there and his parents did too, but tennis won't last forever. I'm pretty sure Harvard will be there if I ever want to try out the college thing."

Jasmine felt the words on her tongue, that it might be something she was going to try, that it might be the best option for her at this point. Playing doubles with Indy might be something she had to give up and soon, but instead, she kept silent as Jack made his way back over to them.

"There is nothing worse than my sister with nothing to do. That poor bastard must be wondering what he saw in her." Indy snorted. It was easy to tell what Alex saw in Penny, though her older brother probably wouldn't see it that way. "It's a good thing we'll be over there soon, before she drives the entire city of London insane."

"We'll be there soon," Indy said, smiling widely. "All of us, at Alex's house, under one roof. Even Teddy."

Jasmine rolled her eyes. "Just a couple of days and we'll be in Wimbledon."

Chapter 6

June 17th

Penny ended the call with Jack and then scanned through her own messages quickly. She moved around, trying to get more comfortable in her seat on the practice court, shifting back and forth on the wooden bench. At least the weather was cool, a fresh spring breeze swirling the London air around her. Alex was scheduled next for this court, but for the last hour, her attention had been solely fixed on the junior American who'd been granted permission by the board at Queens to use their courts for a practice session.

Sixteen-year-old Natalie Grogan, long limbed, with a frizzy brown ponytail and a baby face, was in London for Wimbledon Juniors and from the army of business attire lining the fences, it seemed she was looking for an agent. Penny didn't know much about her except that she beat Jasmine during the French Open junior tournament, and pretty decisively at that, and that Jack had his eye on her as a potential client and had been in contact with her parents. So she'd called her brother and given her two cents, for whatever her opinion on the girl's potential was worth. Her game was solid, no real strength, no real weakness and her playing style actually reminded Penny of her own, doing whatever needed to be done in order to win the match, throwing whatever the opponent sent you back in his or her face, only better.

She watched as the younger girl handed her bags off to her father/coach/manager, and Penny frowned. There was something about girls who didn't carry their own bags that always bothered her, almost as much as parents who insisted on coaching their own kids, but she wiped the frown from her face when Natalie climbed over the low wall separating the stands from the court and headed in her direction.

"Um, hi, you're Penny Harrison, right?" Penny slid her sunglasses off her eyes and placed them up on the bill of her cap. So much for that disguise, as if the walking boot didn't give it away.

"That's me."

"I figured that was you. I mean, I know Alex Russell is scheduled after me so it would just make sense that you were here. I'm Natalie. Um, like, would it be okay if...will you take a picture with me?"

Penny blinked, hoping Natalie would take a breath. She did. "Sure, no problem."

Natalie sat down in the seat beside her and fiddled with her phone before extending her arm out in front of them. They tilted their heads together and Natalie pointed at Penny, feigning a look of surprise before taking the picture. "This is awesome. Nobody would have believed you came to my practice session. You know, like pics or it didn't happen."

"Seriously, no problem," Penny said. "You looked great out there. Keep it up."

"Really? I mean, thanks. I um, I hope your ankle gets better soon. It was amazing, watching you beat Lutrova like that. I couldn't believe it. It was like out of a movie or something, just unbelievable. And now that commercial too, so cool."

There was something about this girl's enthusiasm that made Penny smile. "I couldn't believe it when I first saw it. They didn't even tell me before so it was a complete shock."

"Nat, let's go!" her dad shouted from the court below.

"One second, Dad!" And then to Penny, "Are you gonna play at Wimbledon? They were saying on ESPN that your ankle won't be ready in time. I had a grade 2 sprain once and it sucked. I had to miss Nationals and like all the scouts were there so no one saw me and they were saying before the tournament that I was going to win it and then I had to just sit and watch the whole thing and it just sucked. I really hope you'll be ready." Natalie paused and Penny cut in, the girl's words hitting far too close to home.

"I'll definitely be out there."

"Natalie," her father said, this time making his way up the stairs toward them.

"Good. I can't wait to see you kick Lutrova's ass again." Natalie practically skipped away, tapping at her phone's screen and most likely blasting out the picture. She felt her own phone vibrate in her pocket, notifications that she'd been tagged in the post.

~

Alex and Paolo stepped out onto the court as she scrolled through the alerts on her phone and she saw Natalie dart over in their direction. There was a message from Teddy, her twin brother, that made her smile, *OMG UR SO FAMOUS!11!* It was a running joke in her family to make fun of just how much people would freak out around her sometimes. It still blew her mind that people wanted her autograph or to take a picture with her. Less than a year ago, she hadn't been anyone special and it could just all go away one day. That's why she needed to get back out there, show everyone that she was fine, that she was still the best.

"Hey, you gonna sit all the way up there the whole time?" Alex shouted at her from the court and she rolled her eyes, before standing and slowly making her way down the stairs, the plastic edges of the boot scraping on the concrete. She finally settled on a closer seat.

"You will watch as I destroy him, Penny," Paolo called from the far side of the court.

They weren't really playing a match, just working on different aspects of their games that needed attention in the approach to Wimbledon. Playing on grass was different than playing on clay and you needed time to adjust a little. Time she wouldn't have even if her ankle was ready to go by the first day of the tournament. The pain was manageable now, not nearly as bad as when she first injured it. She could feel pain when her weight was on it, but that wasn't any different from other small injuries she'd had over the years. She just needed to be able to get through matches on it. A fortnight, as they said in this country, would be grueling on a newly healed injury, but she could deal with it if it meant winning her first Grand Slam. She'd been able to fight through the pain in France. Why should England be any different? A little voice in her head, one that sounded suspiciously like her brother Jack's, grumbled the many reasons why not, but she ignored it. She needed to be out on the court in the next few days and that was that.

Alex and Paolo started to hit in earnest and for a minute, Penny watched them, her eyes traveling with the ball back and forth, the satisfying thwap of contact was string music to her ears. And then she let her mind drift, felt the ground beneath her feet, no pain in her ankle, just the soft give of the grass, firmer than the clay she'd just played on in France. She could feel the ball in her hands, fitting perfectly in the cradle of her fingers, one bounce, two, three and four, then lifting her arm up to the sky, pushing her weight down to the ground as the ball rose over her head. Then the racket, slashing through the air, perfect contact, barely feeling the ball leaving the strings over the net, landing balanced, keeping her feet under her and waiting for the return, a crossover step, to a slice back hand down the line, drawing her opponent to one side of the court before taking the next ground stroke and firing it to the opposite court with her forehand for a winner.

By the time she opened her eyes again, she'd played a full match in her head against various opponents in the women's top ten, all with their unique challenges and weaknesses. Women she could come face to face with at Wimbledon, women who were standing in her path to the title. She knew how to beat them all, even when they were at their best. She just had to make sure that *she* was at her best.

"Did you fall asleep over here?" Alex asked, flopping down in the seat beside her and taking a sip from his water bottle, a blue concoction that was supposed to replace electrolytes lost during a practice session.

"Visualizing," she mumbled, a slow smile spreading across her face as he leaned in and pressed a sweaty kiss on her cheek but didn't pull away. He hovered for a moment and let his breath slide over her skin.

"Visualizing, hmm? What's been going through that pretty head of yours, love?"

Penny turned so her lips were just a hair's breadth away from his. "Well, I was thinking about tennis, but now that you mention it…" she trailed off and was about to close the space between them when a catcall made them both jump and pull apart.

"Are we training or not, lover boy?" Paolo called from the court, whacking a ball in their direction.

Alex caught it deftly and stood, grinning, a hand running over his head, sifting through his hair. "Duty calls. Check out my slice serve, would you?" he asked.

"Yeah."

He jogged out to the court and Penny leaned back in her seat with a sigh, settling in to watch. She slipped the walking boot off her foot and the ballet flat off the other before stretching her legs out in the sun. She tried to keep her eyes on him, to check out his slice serve and see what was giving him an issue, but the warmth of the day and the steady rhythm of the ball soon had her eyes drifting closed again. Her opponent was Zina Lutrova this time, like in France, and on grass, Lutrova's game would be even more formidable, the speed of her serve and groundstrokes amped up by the fast surface. Beating her on clay was one thing, but beating her on grass to win Wimbledon, that would be something else entirely.

~

Alex's match that afternoon wasn't much of a challenge. A win, 6-3, 6-4 without need of a third deciding set had them finished at the tournament well before their dinner reservation that night.

"You played well," Penny said, sliding into the back of the car service that would drive them home from the courts.

"No thanks to you," he quipped. "My slice was crap."

"Your slice was fine. I've never been a good coach anyway." She sighed as he lifted her feet and deposited them in his lap, unclasping the boot and letting it fall to the floor of the car. His thumbs massaged the area gently.

"How's that feel?"

Just a few days ago, that area had been extremely sensitive to the touch, the slightest pressure sending spikes of pain through her leg. Now it had faded to almost nothing upon contact and actually felt good, hovering over that borderline between pleasure and pain.

She moaned, leaning her head back against the car window and sliding closer to him as his hands trailed up from her ankles over her calves. "You just played; shouldn't I be giving *you* the massage?"

"Make it up to me later," he murmured as his fingers slipped beneath the skirt of her dress, grazing the inside of her thighs just as the car pulled to a stop in front of his house. The driver's eyes widened in the rear view mirror as they straightened themselves quickly, Penny grabbing her shoe and boot, Alex opening the door and then helping her out. The driver retrieved his bags from the trunk and then sped off into the night.

"I think we shocked him a bit."

Penny laughed as they climbed the stairs and he unlocked the door. "I'm sure he's seen worse."

"Look at that," he said as they climbed the stairs.

"What?" she asked, looking around, seeing nothing but the white townhomes and tree-lined gardens of his street.

"You're not limping."

She glanced down at her feet and smiled. There was only a twinge of pain, nothing crazy, so small she'd barely noticed it as she walked up to the house. Putting all her weight on her *good* foot, she rotated the ankle. "Feels okay."

Alex slung his bag across his back and then swooped in, pulling her into his arms, bridal style, her shriek echoing down the nearly silent street. "Let's keep it that way, shall we? The rest must be doing it good."

"Or you have magical healing powers in your hands."

"I've been saying that for years and finally I've found a girl who believes me."

Kicking the door shut behind him, he carried her into the kitchen and set her down at the kitchen table.

"What time are they expecting us at Cecconi's?" he asked, grabbing a bottle of water from the fridge and then one for her as well, before leaning on the island at the center of the room.

"Seven," she said with a sigh, looking down at her dress, fingering the ends of her windblown hair. "I should change. There'll be cameras and sponsors there tonight."

"Do you really want to go?" he asked, putting down his bottle.

Penny wrung her fingers together as she looked up at him. Was she that easy to read or did he just always know exactly the right thing to say, voicing what she wanted before she even had a chance to do it herself. "If I said I didn't…"

"A night in with you sounds absolutely perfect. I'd spend every night in if I could spend them with you. I love you, Pen."

He'd said those words before, just moments after winning the French Open, but she hardly thought he remembered saying them. Neither of them had mentioned it since, but now the words hung in the air between them and it felt like the first time. No adrenaline, no crowd losing their minds in the background or cameras capturing every moment, just the two of them in his kitchen deciding to stay home rather than head back out into the London night.

Her ankle didn't twinge at all as she stood and crossed the tiled floor or maybe it did and she just didn't care. He offered her his hand and she took it, letting him pull her into his arms, her chest pressing into his as she let herself fall against him. She raised her head and he met her half way, swooping down and sealing his lips over hers, his hands gripping onto his hips and the kiss shifted from soft and sweet, the non-verbal response to his declaration, to something a little different, a little rougher. The scruff of his beard rasping against her skin in that deliciously familiar way.

Sliding her tongue against his, she was suddenly weightless, his hands under her thighs lifting her and spinning quickly, sitting her on the kitchen island, skirt pushed up around her waist. Fingers, calloused from hours upon hours of training danced across her thighs, pulling her to the edge of the counter. Penny reached behind him and tugged at the back of his shirt, pulling the soft cotton over his head before lightly scratching her nails down his back, around his sides and then up over the smooth muscles of his chest.

He groaned into her mouth before pulling away, a hand tilting her neck to just the right angle to run his teeth toward the sensitive skin of her neck. His fingers twined into the chain of the necklace he'd given her in France, the one with the 1936 British penny attached, the one she always wore.

"Like that?" he asked, though he had to know the answer.

Her hands flew to the button of his pants, fumbling with it for a moment before releasing the clasp and pulling down the zipper as he fisted his hands in the skirt of her dress. She lifted up a bit to free the material and as she rose up, bracing herself on his shoulders, a motion just behind them caught her eye. Light brown hair, eyes just like the ones belonging to the man still tugging at her dress and a hand over her mouth. Alex's mother was standing in the doorway.

"Alex," Penny said, tensing; he must have felt it, because he pulled away and then followed her gaze behind them.

"Christ! Mum, what are you doing here?"

Penny slid off the counter and winced as she landed a little awkwardly on her ankle, but more in anticipation of the pain than anything else. She straightened her dress and tried her best to hide a little behind Alex as he pulled his shirt back over his head, sending his hair in all directions.

"I'm so sorry," Anna Russell said, in a soft English accent, different from her son's but Penny couldn't quite pinpoint how. "I thought you two would be gone. I wanted to take back that book I loaned you and I...I am...oh my goodness, my dear, I can't apologize enough. I'm Anna."

She peeked out from over Alex's shoulder and tried to make her feet move, but they felt like she'd just played a five setter. Despite being all the way across the room, it felt like his mother was standing just inches from her, taking in the bite mark on her shoulder and the wrinkles in her dress, the insanity that must be her hair.

"Mum, just give us a minute, okay?"

"Of course," she said and spun around back into the hallway.

"Oh my God," Penny said, her feet finally moving as she paced the small space between the table and the island, back and forth, until Alex's hands on her waist stopped her. "Oh my God, Alex."

"It's fine, Pen. She didn't really see anything and she doesn't care, I promise."

"*I* care. She's your mother and she just saw us almost...oh God."

"Love, you've got to calm down. She's going to love you and this will just be a funny story one day, something to tell the grandkids, eh?"

"You're hilarious. This isn't funny. I wanted her to like me, to know that I wasn't just another..."

"She knows."

"How can...

"Penny, she knows because I told her so. I told her I wanted her to meet you. That she was going to love you, like I do."

"I can't. I just want to die."

"Right, okay. I'm going to go out there and tell her you're too embarrassed to come out, all right? She'll understand."

"She's going to think I'm a coward."

"No, she won't. I know my mum. She's as red as a tomato out there right now too. Gimme a minute."

"It's okay. I'll…I'll come with you."

Penny ran a hand through her hair, smoothed down the line of her dress, straightened her shoulders and took a step forward.

Alex's warm hand slipped into hers. "You're not walking to the gallows, Pen. She's just my mum. Relax."

"Right," she muttered between her teeth as she forced her mouth into a smile. "I can't wait for you to meet my dad."

His hand tightened around hers, but she slipped free as she stepped through the doorway. Her smile became genuine as she heard a murmured, "Fuck," from behind her and the thought that however the next few minutes went, it was going to be easy as pie compared with what her dad would put Alex through.

As soon as they made it into the hallway, they realized it was too late. Alex's mom was gone.

There was a note on the side table, neat scrawl across it. Alex read it and then passed it to her.

So sorry. Still on for dinner tomorrow night. Be safe!

"Your mother thinks I'm a...what do they call it here? A slag."

"Pen, no she doesn't. I promise you. We'll all go out to dinner tomorrow and be laughing about this by the time dessert comes."

Chapter 7

June 18th

Indy was up early. Usually it took two different alarms and multiple snooze buttons to get her out of bed in the morning, but the last few days, her eyes had popped open just before the sun was peaking out over the horizon. In the corner of her room, her bags were stacked neatly. She packed the night before, making sure she had enough clothes to last her the two weeks in London. Penny had texted her strict instructions not to just bring shorts and t-shirts and had even told her to raid her closet if necessary to find some nicer dresses for nights out in the city. She hadn't done it yet, but she'd left some room in her bags to do so after training.

Just a meeting with Dom this morning and a doubles training session with Jasmine and then she had the afternoon off before their early flight the next day. Throwing on some clothes for training, she pocketed her phone and then plugged her earbuds into her ears, letting The Clash's *London Calling* blare through the tiny speakers. Cliché, maybe, but London was calling and it was going to be amazing.

She stepped out into the dorm hallway, lowering the volume just a little, only to hear the door across the hall click shut. Looking up, she met Teddy Harrison's wide eyes head on. Some things never changed. "You're up awfully early," she quipped.

Teddy just rolled his eyes and Indy laughed, but then her eyes caught the sign on the door that hadn't been there the day before. Bright pink bubble letters made out of construction paper that spelled out, *Welcome Back Amy!*

"You didn't," she said, crossing her arms over her chest.

He shrugged, but rubbed a hand across the back of his neck. "I didn't do anything wrong."

Indy huffed and shook her head. "If you don't know why that was a friggin' stupid idea..." She glared at him for another second, before turning to leave.

"Look, just don't say anything to…" he began, but she cut him off, whirling around to face him.

"Jasmine's my friend, Teddy, and if you didn't do anything wrong, then why shouldn't I say anything?" He shifted back and forth on his feet, biting his lip. "Yeah, that's what I thought."

She jogged down the hallway and out the door before he could respond. She had to talk to Jasmine. Should she do it before or after? Definitely after. If she did it before, then it would screw with practice and Dom would be pissed. There were barely any people around yet, just a few of the grounds crew staff prepping the courts for a day's worth of training. The air was warm and light, a soft breeze coming in off the ocean.

"Hey Roy," she called as she entered the atrium, lowering the volume of the music so she could hear him. It was so early, he hadn't even started his paper yet.

"Mornin' Indy," he called, taking a sip of his morning coffee. "You got a meeting with the boss man?"

"Yeah, I'm a little early."

"No worries. That agent of yours went up there a few minutes ago."

"Urg. Great. See you in a bit," she said, raising the volume again, wanting to drown out whatever shouting match Caroline and Dom would inevitably be having when she got up to his office.

She took the stairs two at a time, keeping her eyes on the steps, not wanting to twist her ankle doing something as stupid as going to a meeting with her coach. The papers on the floor of Dom's office should have been the first clue. Brightly colored folders, normally stacked neatly on the desk were scattered on the shiny wood floor, their contents strewn around them, except her eyes were drawn to the glare of the sun rising in the distance through the floor-to-ceiling windows of the office, blinding her as she reached the top of the stairway. That and the music blaring from her earphones probably drowned out the sounds that would have alerted her to what was happening just past the top of the stairs, so apparently, it was her destiny to jog into her coach's office for their weekly progress meeting only to find him with his pants around his ankles. At first, her brain didn't quite understand what she was seeing, so she just kept looking, past the horror of Dom's naked ass to the blonde hair, usually so perfectly coiffed into a twist or a knot in complete disarray, long, pale legs wrapped around his waist.

"Holy shit." Her voice was a lot louder than she meant for it to be, the music pounding through her earbuds forcing her voice up in volume.

The couple on the desk froze and she locked eyes with Caroline over Dom's shoulder, seeing her agent's lips form the word, Indiana. Dom started to fumble to pull his pants up and turn around, but Indy spun on her toes and raced down the stairs. She hit a full sprint two steps into the atrium, flying past Roy at the security desk. He actually dropped his paper in concern, but she was through the doors and out into the open air before he could even shout her name. She felt her phone buzzing in her pocket, probably Dom or Caroline, maybe both, but her stride didn't break as she flew down the street toward the Harrison house.

~

Pounding on the door, probably harder than necessary, she yanked the earbuds out of her ears, the sound of guitar and screechy vocals fading to a buzz before reaching up to knock again, just catching herself before she wacked Teddy in the face with her fist.

"Hey," he began, but she flew past him, her long legs taking the stairs two at a time, skidding down the hallway and storming straight into Jack's bedroom, slamming the door behind her.

"Indy?" he rasped, rubbing his eyes with the heel of his hands.

"I just…I just saw," she tried to breathe in through her nose and back out through her mouth to catch her breath and finally it worked. Sitting down on the edge of his bed, she continued to breathe slowly; the feel of his legs behind her, even through the layers of covers, was a comfort.

"What did you see?" he asked, sitting up fully, the sheet pooling at his waist, but even the sight of him shirtless wasn't enough to erase the horrible image from her mind.

"Dom and Caroline. They were, oh God, they were on his desk and I think I'm going to throw up." She covered her face with her hands as her stomach twisted in revulsion.

Jack pulled his legs from beneath the covers and twisted around to sit beside her, his thigh lining up with hers. "Breathe, baby, breathe. You walked in on them?"

"Having sex on his desk. Dom's ass hanging out. I'm never going to get that image out of my head."

"Indiana," Jack started but she cut him off.

"What do I do? Do I tell my Dad? I have to tell him, don't I? I mean, this is huge. She's cheating on him. My agent and my coach. My dad's girlfriend and my coach. This is, this is just way too much. What do I do?" she asked again. "Should I fire her? I mean, this is something you fire an agent over right? Like, a *huge* conflict of interest."

"You want my advice?" He took her hand in his. "First, you need to calm down a little. Making decisions right now, it's a bad idea. Let's just sit here for a second and breathe."

He leaned back against his pillows, pulling her with him and she curled up into his chest. One of his arms snaked around her waist, holding her close, the other stroked her hair, twisting the ends around his fingers before letting the curls untwine themselves. "You okay?"

"Yeah," she said, breathing in his scent. Letting the warmth of his skin ease the tension in her body. "I just. What do I do? What would you do?"

"We're not talking about me. What do *you* want to do?"

"I want to fire her ass and then tell my dad his girlfriend is cheating scum. And I'm so pissed off at Dom."

"You have a right to be pissed, baby, but look, I've learned something over the last couple of years in this business. It's a small world and everyone's got a lot of baggage, everyone knows everyone, everyone is connected. The best way to navigate it is to keep business and personal separate. So Caroline is sleeping with your coach and cheating on your dad. She makes bad personal decisions. Does any of that mean she's not a great agent?"

"No."

"And Dom, does this mean he's not still the best coach in the world?"

"No."

"Would you want to train with anyone else?"

"Definitely not."

"Then okay. You still have one of the best agents in the world, present company excluded, of course, and the best coach in the world. Even if you want to throttle them, is staying with both of them what's best for your career?"

"Probably," she grumbled, annoyed at how reasonable he was about this. "You could be my agent though."

"Baby, I can't even tell you how bad an idea that is."

"Yeah?" She turned her head, her lips brushing the skin of his shoulder, goosebumps rising as her mouth curved into a smile.

"Oh yeah. What's happening between us, it's special and I don't want it to get messy. Messier than it already is anyway. Let's keep this," he squeezed her hip firmly, "and everything else separate."

"But what about my dad?"

"That's the tough one. Do you want to tell him?"

She didn't hesitate. "Yes."

"Then call him. Tell him and your conscience is clear."

She pulled her phone from her pocket, the missed calls and voicemails from her coach and her agent lined up on her screen, but she flicked past them and brought up her Dad's number.

Jack slipped from beneath her. "I'll be right outside," he whispered and shut the door behind him.

~

She dialed the number and she could barely catch her breath, her heart nearly pounding out of her chest cavity, her throat tight and her stomach spinning circles in her gut, all the serenity from those moments with Jack completely gone. The phone rang and rang, over and over again. He was abroad, in China, and she knew it would head to voicemail, knew she'd hear her father's voice saying his own name and then the computerized woman telling her to leave a message, but then there was a click and it connected.

"Indiana?" Charles Gaffney's voice echoed loud and clear through the strong cell service.

Indy blinked. She didn't know he had her number in his phone. "Hi Dad," she managed to croak out.

"Indiana, is anything wrong?"

"Um, why, why would you ask that?" she asked, her voice cracking a little.

"You never call me," he said, "I can't imagine why...is there something wrong? Are you okay?" The words were completely foreign to her.

Your girlfriend, my agent, is sleeping with my coach. She's cheating on you. The words were easy in her head, but she couldn't force them past the lump in her throat. She didn't even know why it was so tough. It should have been simple. Just tell him and hang up. Get it over with, except the words were just friggin' stuck and wouldn't budge, not for anything.

"Indiana?"

"No, um, nothing's wrong. I'm fine. I just thought I'd call. You know, to um, catch up."

"Catch up?" he repeated. Apparently it had sounded just as stupid to him as it had to her.

"Yeah, we just…we don't really talk, like you said, ever, and I…if you're busy, I understand, it's fine. I'm sure you're busy."

He cleared his throat sharply. "I am, but I can—"

"No, it's okay," she said, seeing her escape and taking it. "We'll…we can talk later. No big deal. Bye."

She ended the call and clenched her fist around the phone. Hauling back her arm, she nearly threw it across the room, but stopped herself as the phone began to buzz in her hand. Without even looking at the screen, she answered it.

"Hello?"

"You didn't let me finish. I was just about to go into a meeting, but I cancelled it. Now, I can tell something's wrong, India—Indy. You wouldn't call me unless you had no other option, I know that much. Now let me know what it is and maybe I can help."

She hadn't expected him to call back, let alone for him to talk to her like that, like what happened to her mattered or that his concern wasn't simply because he *had* to be concerned. Indy tried to get the words to form on her lips again, but still, they wouldn't come. How do you tell someone something like that, especially your dad, especially Charles Gaffney? "It's nothing. I just…does Caroline *have* to be my agent? I know you and her are a thing, but…"

A heavy sigh echoed through the speaker. She couldn't tell if it was in relief or exasperation. "Caroline is the best at what she does. Even if she and I weren't *a thing,* as you say, I'd still want her to represent your interests."

"I don't trust her."

"Has she ever done anything to betray your trust?"

"She didn't tell me that you guys were together."

"Indy, do you tell her about your boyfriends?"

"I don't have a boyfriend, but even if I did, that's different," she protested, biting her lip after the words flew out a little too fast and a little too high pitched.

She could almost hear the laugh in her dad's voice as he said, "You're right, it is different. Your personal relationships could have a potential impact on her ability to perform her job. Hers do not. What I'm trying to say is that you don't have to like her. It's not personal. It's *business* and it would be a silly business decision to let the best tennis agent in the world go because of something *personal.*" It was almost exactly what Jack said. Apparently, the two most important men in her life had a lot more in common than she'd ever imagined.

"What about the opposite?"

There was a long pause on the other end. "Letting business get in the way of personal things?"

"Yes."

And with that word, they weren't talking about Caroline anymore. They were talking about the missed birthdays and Christmases and phone calls never returned and gifts picked out by secretaries. It was about them.

"Then...then you have to decide what's more important to you," he said, finally, but slowly, like it wasn't really what he wanted to say, even though it was the truth. A truth that hit her hard, right in the chest. He'd always put his business before personal, always put his job before her and her mom, because he'd decided a long time ago that business was more important than them.

"Right, okay, sure."

"Indiana, that doesn't mean..."

"I've gotta go."

She ended the call, hearing the line disconnect, but she kept the phone to her ear. "Caroline is cheating on you with my coach, but whatever, I don't even care, you and her, you deserve each other. You're the kind of people who don't care about who you hurt. You don't care and now I don't care either. You both can go to hell." Then she took a deep breath and chucked the friggin' phone against the wall as hard as she could.

Chapter 8

June 18th

Jasmine felt her feet sink into the sand, sneakers pushing the grains away as she headed for the shoreline behind her parents' house. Her racket bag was slung over her back, the strap across her chest and she was dressed for training. She had a doubles session with Indy in about a half hour and a run on the beach always helped to clear her head beforehand. It also had the added bonus of getting her out of the house before her parents woke up. Avoiding them was becoming an art form. She would be gone before they got out of bed, spend the entire day at OBX and then would creep back into the house after the sun set. They were leaving for London tomorrow so she only had to keep it up for one more day.

The shoreline was damp from high tide, leaving the sand wet with just enough give to make running comfortable. She set a slow pace, not needing to wear herself out before the day really began and let her mind just go blank. None of the crap that went down this week mattered. Not really. They were flying to London tomorrow. She and Indy were going to qualify for doubles and they were going to kick ass. Training was going better than ever. Their physical games had always complemented each other, but now, they were on the same page mentally and there were times when they barely had to speak on the court. Soon enough, that would become the norm and they'd be unstoppable.

Only a few people were buzzing around the OBX grounds when she got to their practice court, but Dom was one of them, waiting with three junior boys who would be their opponents. Canadian Doubles, the training regimen Dom had instituted a few days before was making practice extreme but would pay off once they got on the court with the best in the world.

"Hey kiddo," Dom said, as she rounded the corner of the court and slipped through the gate.

A quick glance around the empty court had her turning to Dom. "I'm guessing you didn't just give Indy the day off, right?"

"Nah, she's got a conflict this morning."

"A conflict?" That made absolutely no sense. Indy wouldn't miss training for anything. "Is everything okay?"

"It's fine. She'll be on the flight with us tomorrow. She just needs a day."

Sounded like a bunch of bullshit, but Jasmine let it go. She'd talk to Indy later. "Okay, so then, what are we doing?"

"I moved up your singles training session and invited Fitz to play a set."

She pulled her racket back off her back and laid it against the fence. "She's late."

"No, I'm right on time," Amy said, slinging an arm around her neck and bumping their hips together. "Dominic."

"Morning, Fitz. Okay, both of you, a couple of circuits around the court and then warm up."

"How long has it been, Jazzy?" Amy asked as they started their jog, rotating their arms in slow circles to loosen up.

"Since we played against each other? The OBX semi-final two years ago, I guess."

Amy threw her head back and laughed. "That's right. That was a good match."

"If by good match you mean kicking my ass, then yeah, it was a good match."

"Aw, it was closer than the score line."

"It really wasn't. Didn't really matter though. Penny destroyed you in the final."

"And then she destroyed you the two years after that."

"Ladies, this isn't social hour. Talk on your own time," Dom snapped from the edge of the court.

Jasmine jogged away without another word, grabbing her racket.

"Volley for serve, Jazzy?" Amy asked, taking the side of the court with her back to the beach, ensuring that Jasmine would have the sun rising in her eyes for at least the first game.

"Nah, it's all yours," Jasmine said, slipping her sunglasses on, the polarized lenses negating the affects of the sun.

"Sure about that?" Amy sounded pretty confident. She was a two-time, All-American and had once been the best OBX had to offer.

Jasmine was going to make sure she understood. A lot had changed in two years. "Positive."

The grass courts at OBX were normally like a ghost town, with most of the athletes spending their practice time on the hard courts, but word travelled quickly and by the time they were done with their warm-ups, a small crowd of people who had nowhere better to be lined the courts to watch the Academy's first two athletes go head to head again after so long.

The buzz around them quieted a bit as they took their positions at the baseline. When she was young, before Dom had started her on a truly rigorous elite level conditioning program, Jasmine had always been the weaker player, her physical strength unequal to a girl's a few years older than her. That wouldn't be the case this morning. Jasmine had spent the two years since training against the likes of Penny Harrison and Indiana Gaffney, playing on Chatrier at Roland Garros against the best doubles players in the world, the Kapur twins, forcing them to a third set. She wasn't that little girl who got her as kicked in the OBX semifinal anymore. Not by a long shot. Amy's game had always been a solid one, no real weakness and her strengths, a solid backhand and decent forehand, worked great against NCAA competition but wouldn't compare to the level of play Jasmine faced down on a regular basis.

Jasmine bounced up and down on the balls of her feet, and then landed, legs spread just a little more than shoulder width apart, her weight shifting back and forth. Amy tossed the ball and served it straight and flat, skipping through the center of the service box. Landing balanced led to a quick crossover step and then a strong forehand had the ball rocketing back over the net into the corner of the deuce court before Amy had recovered enough to return it.

Amy stood still at the baseline, staring at where the ball had bounced, but there was no doubt it was in, a clean winner. The crowd buzzed around them and Jasmine let her eyes flicker over the faces, catching Teddy standing off to the side, leaning against the fence, a smirk lifting the corner of his mouth. Amy stepped into her line of sight and raised her eyebrows over the net, but Jasmine shrugged, moving to the other side of the service line.

The next serve, Amy tried to send out wide, but she missed beyond the doubles alley and Jasmine sent the ball back to her and waited for the second serve. Jasmine took a few steps in, a clear sign to the crowd around her just how little respect she had for Amy's serves. The older girl saw where she was standing, paused and let the ball fall again, bouncing it against her racket and shifting her feet a little. Another toss and Amy sent her next serve closer to the line, but Jasmine was on it almost before it bounced, lining up the backhand and ripping it cross-court. Amy managed to get a racket on it, but Jasmine shuffled closer to the net and finished the point with a short volley. The crowd buzzed again, but this time, Jasmine ignored them all.

Standing at the baseline with her hands propped on her hips, her racket hanging limply in one hand, Jasmine tilted her head. Amy pouted and let out a begrudging sniff. Clearly, the match wasn't going quite the way she had planned.

Twenty minutes later, Dom called a halt to things and the crowd milled around for a while, the chatter carrying out over the court to Jasmine as she gulped down her Gatorade.

"Did Fitz totally lose it in California?"

"Nah, Jasmine just destroyed her."

Grabbing a towel and shielding her face with it, she smiled into the rough terrycloth and then wiped the sheen of sweat off her forehead.

"Nice set, Jazzy," Amy said, grabbing her own drink. "Didn't know you had it in you."

"Yeah, we should do it again sometime."

"Definitely."

Jasmine turned her back and tossed her drink into her racket bag, knowing she would never have to face Amy Fitzpatrick on a tennis court again.

~

The locker room was virtually empty when Jasmine stepped out of the shower. Morning sessions were all in full swing and she dressed in peace and quiet, the adrenaline still thrumming through her veins from the win. She had the afternoon off. All she had to do was head home and finish packing, then tomorrow morning, they'd be on a plane to London. Penny had texted everyone that Alex was inviting them all to stay at his London townhouse for the duration of the tournament. He had more than enough space and it would be nice to be away from the constant scrutiny of the major tournament hotels. She and Indy would have to share one of the four bedrooms since his training partner Paolo Macchia was staying there as well, but there would be enough room for Jack and Teddy too. It would be a crazy few weeks all crammed together in one house, but it would be a blast.

She stored her rackets in her locker and headed out into the bright sunshine of the North Carolina spring, a rare day to spend with nothing to do except relax.

"Hey Jazzy," Amy called from just outside the door, leaning against the fence of a practice court with Teddy Harrison at her side.

Jasmine clenched her teeth together at the ridiculous nickname. She thought maybe the defeat on the court would mellow out Amy's obnoxiousness, but apparently it didn't.

"Hey guys."

"Teddy was just saying he'd take me to Deuce for breakfast so we can catch up before y'all leave for London. Isn't that sweet of him?"

"So sweet," Jasmine agreed, looking at Teddy, who refused to make eye contact with her.

Amy wrapped her hand around Teddy's forearm, leaning into him, her breasts brushing against his bicep. It could have been innocent contact, but Jasmine knew Amy better than that. What really annoyed her was that Teddy wasn't pulling away. "Oh my God, you should totally come with us. We can reminisce about the glory days."

She'd rather spork her eyes out and feed them to the seagulls circling overhead.

"Jasmine has stuff to do, don't you?" Teddy answered for her.

"Lots of stuff," she agreed, but he shifted back and forth, his shoulders wilting under the weight of her glare. It wasn't like she was going to accept the invitation, but the last thing she needed was Teddy to speak for her. "Getting ready for Wimbledon, you know. We'll catch up when we all come back."

Amy stuck out her lower lip and slid her hand down Teddy's arm, interlocking their fingers together. "No way. Dom said you had the rest of the day off at the end of our match and I know you, you've been packed for days. Come with us, please?"

That's how she found herself at Deuce in the middle of the morning, listening to Amy wax poetic about how amazing it was in Palo Alto and how Stanford was everything she hoped it would be.

"I can't believe you chose Duke, Ted. You would love Cali."

"Wanted to be near family," he said around a mouthful of eggs. He'd been stuffing his face with food since they sat down, letting Amy's mouth run to her heart's content and he hadn't even glanced at Jasmine once since they sat down.

"Yeah, but your family isn't going to be here. I mean, your mom and dad yes, but Penny and Jack are going to be all over the world and you're going to be stuck here in North Carolina with all the little OBXers."

"Duke is an amazing school and they have a great tennis team," Jasmine cut in.

"You'll have to come out and visit on breaks then."

Teddy pulled his phone out, alerts popping out on his screen as he flicked his thumb over it. He flicked his eyes to Amy and then glanced quickly at the door. "I gotta go. Jack's freaking out 'cause I didn't find my passport yet. See you guys later."

He was up from the table before either of them could utter a word of protest.

"So you and Teddy, again?" Jasmine asked, before he'd even left the restaurant.

Amy was watching him leave. "There's just something about that boy, you know? Like a magnet. His older brother too, but Jack wouldn't go after his little bro's ex, that much is obvious."

"So you're just hooking up with him because Jack's not an option? Nice, Amy," she said, unable to keep the bitterness out of her voice and she cringed as Amy's eyes lit up.

"Oh my God, you guys *did* hook up, didn't you?"

"About a month ago," Jasmine mumbled, already sorry she said anything.

"Wow. I mean he mentioned that things got a little weird between you, but I didn't realize. You don't mind, do you? I mean, of course you don't. He's my ex-boyfriend. You probably should be asking me if I mind or apologizing. That's a big no-no in the Girl Code, but whatever, I guess it's over now since you're clearly not together."

"Clearly not," Jasmine repeated. "We decided we're better off as friends."

"Both of you or just him?"

"Both of us," she said quickly.

Amy's eyes grew wide, but the small upward motion of her mouth betrayed her amusement. "Oh, you are upset, aren't you? I'm sorry, Jazzy."

"Don't be. I'm not upset. You're welcome to Teddy Harrison."

The smile widened. "Good, because I have plans for him. Now let's get down to business."

"Business?"

"You really think I asked you to breakfast to talk about Teddy? Come on, Jazzy."

"Could you not call me that?"

Amy laughed, waving her hand in the air dismissively. "Why? I've always called you that. Anyway, look, my coach wanted me to talk to you about coming to Stanford in the fall."

Jasmine arched a brow and shook her head. "I don't think that's a good idea."

"Why not? I know the college scouts have been circling and you haven't gone pro yet for a reason, let's be honest. You're so not ready. You'd be great on our team. Think about it. Me and you, number one and two singles."

"More like two and one," she muttered and then shook her head. "If your coach is that interested, tell her to call my parents. They're the ones handling all that crap."

Amy grinned widely. "Awesome."

"Yeah, awesome. Look, I've gotta go. I want to check on Indy and then I promised my parents we'd spend some time together before I leave." Jasmine stood, walking away much the same way Teddy had just a few minutes ago.

"See you when you get back, Jazz," Amy called. She didn't have to look back to see the smug smile still plastered across the stupid bitch's face.

"Can't wait."

She was just out of Deuce and headed toward the beach when she saw Indy's blonde hair rounding the corner headed toward the dorms, a swathe of glittering cloth over her arm.

"Where were you?" Jasmine said as soon as she was in earshot.

Indy looked behind her, like she might be speaking to someone else. "I had to, I…"

"Please don't tell me you skipped training to pick out a dress."

"No, I was at Jack's and I grabbed this before I left, but…"

"So you skipped training to make out with Jack?" Jasmine nearly screeched.

"Keep your voice down," Indy said, looking around to make sure they were still alone, but nearly everyone was at training. "No, there was a thing with my Dad and I had to…I had to take care of it and Jack helped."

Jasmine's anger faded immediately and was replaced with concern. "Your Dad?" She knew

Indy couldn't stand her father. "Is everything okay?"

Indy nodded, rolling her eyes. "Yeah, everything is fine. The same, you know, but fine."

"Are you sure?"

"Yeah, I'm sorry I had to miss training."

"It's fine. You missed me kicking Amy Fitzpatrick's ass, but…"

"You did *what*?"

"It was awesome."

"Tell me everything."

"Dom decided to let us play a set in place of doubles training. It was *awesome*. She couldn't keep up. Just kept hitting the ball back to me and letting me dictate everything. I remember her being so much better than that."

"She's probably the same. You got better. It's been what? Two years?"

"Made me think about what Dom said."

"What did Dom say?"

"Oh um, he…well he said that if I decided to go to school in the fall, NCAA wouldn't be…I'd be, the best I guess?"

"Are you considering that?"

"I have to, kind of, don't I? I mean it's a great option."

"I guess so. I just thought…"

"What?"

"I didn't think college was something you were thinking about, that's all."

"It's mostly my parents. They brought it up when we got back from Paris."

"By when would you have to decide?"

"It's already pretty late, but I guess there are some schools that are interested."

"Stanford?" Indy said, a shit-eating grin spreading across her face.

"Yeah, that's not going happen. I don't really want to think about it until after Wimbledon. We've got a lot of work to do in London and this is just a distraction."

"Well, you know where I stand on it."

"Do I?"

"We got a taste of it in France. Could you really go play in the NCAA after that? I couldn't."

"Maybe we're different."

"I don't think we are." Jasmine snorted. "Fine, but we're not *that* different at least. You want to be the best."

"I would be the best there."

"Yeah, but not in the world."

Jasmine shook her head. "Whatever. I still have time and Jack said…"

"You talked to Jack about this?" Indy cut her off.

Wincing, Jasmine nodded. "I'm sorry. I asked him not to say anything."

"Is that why you guys were talking about Harvard?"

"Yeah."

They lapsed into silence. Jasmine didn't know what else to say. She was sorry she hadn't told Indy to begin with, but there wasn't anything to tell at first. Really, there still wasn't. It was just an option, something to keep in the back of her head. The sun caught on the sparkly material still draped over Indy's arm.

"Been in Penny's closet?" she guessed, changing the subject.

"Yeah. I was going to go over there anyway later, but I figured it was easier just to let Teddy think that I was grabbing a dress instead of going to see Jack. I mean, we didn't do anything, but he doesn't know and…"

"Indy, it's fine. I get it. You two should come clean soon though. It's got to be exhausting to keep it all a secret."

"In London. We decided to tell everyone in London."

"That's good. I can't wait to get out of here. If I have to watch that bitch sink her claws into Teddy again…"

"Wait. What?"

"Amy. She was all over him at breakfast today and he wouldn't even look at me. It's like it's happening all over again."

"It is."

"What do you mean?"

"He asked me not to say anything, but this morning, when I came out of my room, Teddy was sneaking out of hers."

Jasmine felt her heart twist and she tried to muster some shock, but she wasn't all that surprised. "He's such an idiot."

"Well, clearly."

"No, you don't get it. You weren't here when she broke up with him. She basically destroyed him. He didn't speak to anyone for weeks. Then all of a sudden, he was at a beach party slobbering all over some girl's face and laughing like nothing happened. Then after the match today, she dragged me along on their breakfast to 'catch up' like some third wheel and he just went along with it, like she's got some kind of spell over him."

Indy tilted her head. "First loves have a weird kind of power over us like that. You know that better than anyone."

"I do?"

"Why else did you go to breakfast with them, Jas?"

"Crap."

Chapter 9

June 18th

Alex was already up and moving around the bedroom when Penny opened her eyes. She could hear him opening and closing drawers in his dresser and digging through the mess on top of his nightstand to find his watch. Just like every morning lately, her first instinct was to point her toes and then rotate her ankle. She waited for the pain, the dull ache that accompanied the movement, but there was nothing, just her ankle twisting in a circle one way and then the other, but no pain, not even a twinge. Spinning her legs out from under the covers and planting her feet firmly on the floor, she waited again, pushing a little at the injury. Nothing. So, she stood up, making sure to keep her weight evenly balanced and then leaned her full body to the injured side. The tiniest of twinges, but then it held strong.

"Alex," she said, staring at the joint, not sure if she was still dreaming.

"Yeah, love?" he called back distractedly.

"Would you mind if I took up some of your practice time today?"

"What?" He spun around, his hair still sticking up from the night's sleep. "Are you sure?"

"It feels…" she trailed off, rotating the ankle again to make sure. "It feels good." Or at least it felt better than it had since she hurt it.

Alex crossed the room and tapped her shoulder, guiding her back to the bed. Kneeling in front of her, he took her leg in his hand, cupping her foot by the heel. His thumb pressed into the joint, increasing the pressure and looking up at her for a reaction. She just shook her head, her smile growing with every moment she didn't feel pain.

Leaning forward, she took his face in her hands. "I'm training today," she said before brushing her lips over his.

His hands came up to cover hers and he squeezed gently. "You're going to stretch and wrap it tight and take it easy, but yeah, you're gonna train. My mum is going to meet up with you before the final tonight, so no overdoing it and using that as an excuse to get out of it."

"Me? Never." she said and he ran a finger up the bottom of her foot, one of her few ticklish spots. She fell back onto the bed and let out a squeal, pulling her foot away. Alex came with her, landing on his side, propping himself up on his elbow.

"Dom's gonna kill me for letting you work out without him."

"Dom's a big boy. He'll get over it."

"You promise me you'll take it easy."

"Promise."

"You want me to hit with you?"

"Nah, you need to put in a tough workout. I know exactly who to call."

As soon as she walked out onto the Queens practice courts, it was pretty obvious that word had spread about her taking up part of Alex's hitting session. Reporters were lining the edge of the court, kept back by the fences and security. Photographers had their cameras poised, looking for any sign of weakness, a limp, a grimace of pain, anything to write about and call into question her chances of winning Wimbledon.

"Penny," Natalie Grogan said, jogging up to her as she stepped onto the court.

"Hey, glad you could make it."

"Oh my God, of course! I was so excited when my dad told me you called."

"You ready to get started?"

She had stretched out fully in the trainer's room after getting her ankle wrapped up tight, so she was pretty much ready to go and didn't want to waste any more of Alex's practice time than necessary.

"Let's do it. Just moving around the court a little bit, get some serves in, baseline and then net work."

"Sounds good to me!"

The grass was a little slick after a few days of the tournament players using it far more than the usual club members, but it felt good under her feet, solid and a little cushioning. Natalie was a good player, a little rough around the edges still, but they gave each other a decent workout. She tried to put her ankle out of her mind, but as they crept close to the hour and a half they'd agreed on, she began to feel it twinge as she worked through her serving arsenal, growing a little worse with each impact. It was only the first day, so Penny felt pretty good about how long it held up. She waved Natalie to the net.

"That's good for now."

Natalie's face fell a little bit, but then she brightened again, racing to her racket bag and pulling out her phone. "Can we do another selfie?"

"As long as you don't mind us looking like a sweaty mess," Penny said with a laugh.

"Please, I'm always a sweaty mess."

"Me too, up until recently. It's actually nice to feel like this again."

"Are you kidding? You always look fabulous. *Seventeen* had this whole thing about your off-court style. Flawless."

Penny grabbed her phone and held it out, tilting her head toward the other girl. "Okay, stupidest face you can imagine," she said, twisting her mouth into a snarl and crossing her eyes. Natalie blew her cheeks up like a balloon and they snapped the pic. "Okay and now duck face." They pursed their lips and took another selfie.

"Awesome." Natalie took her phone back. "How's your ankle feeling?"

Glancing down at it, Penny shrugged. "Wrapped so tight I don't even know. I'll ice it and see how it feels later tonight."

"If you need another hitting partner, just give me a call. I mean, I know you'll probably want to hit with Indiana Gaffney when she gets here tomorrow. She's like your best friend, right? But I thought she might be busy because she's playing doubles qualifying with Jasmine Randazzo and then the juniors too, so if you need anyone, I'd love to help out."

"You'll be my first call, Nat. Promise."

"Great! Oh, and is your brother coming tomorrow too? The blogs were saying that the OBX girls were, but they didn't say anything about Jack and my dad wanted to talk to him about some business stuff, I think."

Penny brightened. She knew Jack had had his eye on Natalie for a little while as a possible client, but up until this week, she hadn't given any indication that she planned on signing with an agent. He'd be thrilled. She made a mental note to text him from the trainer's room. "He'll be here tomorrow too. Hopefully, they can get together."

"Yeah, that'd be awesome. I'll see you later."

Penny showered quickly and pulled on her favorite white eyelet dress, letting her hair air dry, the dark brown curls falling down her back, completing the look with brown leather flip flops, gold metal fixtures near the toes that wouldn't interfere with her ankle wrap.

~

"Well done," Anna Russell said as Penny took the seat next to her at the edge of the practice court.

"Thanks. It's nice to get back out on the court."

"How does your ankle feel?"

Penny glanced down at the large ice pack wrapped securely around her foot, numbing the joint. "I can't feel it right now, but it'll be sore tonight. Shouldn't be too bad though. Not like it was in France."

"It was extraordinary, what you did there. I was on the edge of my seat for that last game. I haven't felt that way during a tennis match in a long time. Not even when Alex was playing."

"Thank you."

She didn't know what else to say and the silence hung in the air like a dead man at the end of a noose. Death a foregone conclusion, just the agony of waiting for it to happen remained.

Thankfully, Anna knew how to make small talk. She pushed through the awkwardness like one of her son's serves. "How do you like London so far?"

"Haven't really seen much of it. Just the airport, the courts and Alex's house."

"You've been here before though, haven't you?"

"Last year for juniors."

"Which you won. Rather spectacularly, if I recall."

"I did." She didn't know Alex's mom had seen her play before.

"I can't wait to see you play in the main draw this year. Even taking away my new bias in your direction, you've been one of my favorite players to watch for some time now. Truly."

"Thank you."

The conversation stalled again. Penny never felt like this before, there were no words, nothing to say that wouldn't be completely mortifying. They watched Alex continue his warm-ups, he and Paolo trading groundstrokes and keeping up a verbal sparring match at the same time. Their usual routine, half in English, half in Italian and mostly aspersions on everything about the other, none of which were taken the least bit seriously.

"Penny, you don't have to be embarrassed around me, sweetheart."

The tension broke and Penny chewed on her lower lip before responding. "Yes, I really do."

"You think that's the first time I've walked in on Alex and one of his girlfriends?"

"That's the thing, I don't care what the press thinks or what other people think, but I don't want to be *one of his girlfriends*. Not to you."

"You're not."

"Feels like it. I mean, not that you made me feel that way, just that… I don't even know what I'm saying."

Anna placed a hand on top of the fingers Penny was twisting together so hard they were beginning to turn purple. "You're not. He made us dinner reservations for tonight so we could get to know each other. Do you know how many girls my son has asked me to go to dinner with, to even have a conversation with, to meet at all?"

"No."

"One. You. Just you."

"Oh."

"Oh, indeed. I've never been thrilled with the women Alex has been with in the past, but he's a grown man and he's been making his own decisions for a long time. Since he was a little boy, really. You, my dear, are one of the best decisions he has ever made. The change in him, I swear."

"Change?"

"You might love my son, Penny, but you don't know him. Not really, not yet. He is different and it is clearly because of you."

"I…"

"It's not a bad thing. I haven't seen him this happy in a very long time. Years."

"And you think that's because of me? He just won the French Open. He's going to win Wimbledon again. I don't…"

"A mother knows."

"Knows what?"

"When her son's found the woman he's supposed to be with for the rest of his life." Penny let the words sink in and didn't respond for a moment and then another. Anna reached out and took her hand. "I'm sorry, was that too much?"

"No." Her voice cracked a little. "No, it wasn't and I think — I think that's what's scary."

"Let me guess, this wasn't part of your plan?"

"No, I…tennis is — was everything."

"For him too, since he was just yea high," she said, lining her hand up with her thigh. "I enrolled him in anything that would keep him busy enough to tire him out. Football, cricket, basketball. Tennis was the only thing that stuck."

"Didn't play well with others?"

"Well spotted. He liked boxing too, but I put a stop to that."

"I was the same way. I hated relying on other people to help me win."

"You two are so different and yet so alike. You have tennis, your family, your friends," she nodded out toward the court, "and now each other."

"I think that's why it works."

"I think so too."

"I'm so sorry that was the first impression you got of me. I know you say it's not a big deal, but it is to me. I don't…that's not something I take lightly. I fought it for a long time. Too long, maybe, but you have to know, I do love him, very much."

"Sweetheart, I think that's pretty clear and I'm sorry too."

"For what?"

"For not knocking."

Anna laughed lightly and nudged Penny a little and though she fought it for a moment, her laughter was contagious.

"This can't be good. I don't need you two teaming up," Alex said, tossing himself into the seat beside Penny, pressing a sweaty kiss against her temple. "Everything all right?" he whispered against her hair so his mother couldn't hear. She squeezed his arm gently in a silent "yes."

"You're doomed," Anna said, smiling widely at her son. "Outnumbered from here on out, darling."

"Your mother was just telling me about when you were little."

Alex groaned dramatically, burying his face in her shoulder, his scruff scraping against the skin before he pressed a soft kiss there. "Okay, back to it. Mum don't give away all my secrets. Penny already knows too much about me, any more and she might bolt."

"I don't know," Anna said, smiling widely. "I think she might be here to stay. Lord help her."

"You both ready to watch me kick some ass?"

"Absolutely," Penny said, lacing her fingers through his and letting him pull her up from the seat.

~

Penny and Anna were ushered to front row seats at the Queens center court. It was much more intimate than the center courts at the Grand Slams. The clubhouse lined one side of the court and temporary seating along the club's famous trellis added a second viewing level. The other side of the court was long, sloped theater seating, providing a great view even from the worst seats. A lottery had been held months earlier to decide who would receive tickets, much like the one held for Wimbledon, club members of course taking priority over the rest of the public.

"Have you seen his opponent before?" Anna asked as they settled into their seats, the rest of the crowd still milling around, waiting for the players to appear. There was still a week before the Championships at Wimbledon, but tennis season was in full swing in England and the buzz was beginning to feel electric leading up to this final.

"Makhassè Vargas," Penny said, "from Bolivia. Ranked twenty-sixth in the world. Mostly tries to hit from the baseline, but his game isn't quite up to that level. Alex shouldn't have a problem."

Anna laughed softly. "Do you scout the men's side too?"

"I may have eavesdropped on his Skype call with Dom this morning."

"So what you're saying is that we shouldn't have a problem keeping our nine o'clock reservation?"

Penny checked her watch. It was nearly seven, the early summer sun still shining brightly, no thought of setting for a while yet. "I'm saying we might be a little early."

"Good. I haven't been able to sit down with Alex for a meal in far too long. And now, since you and Dom both seem to think this match won't be worthy of our attention, tell me about you, my dear. Start from the beginning."

"The beginning?" Penny said, shrugging. "Well, I was born in Chicago…"

Chapter 10

June 19th

Heathrow Airport was an utter mad house, living up to its reputation as one of Europe's busiest airports. Indy had been there as a child, but she didn't have any clear memories of it other than holding tight to her mother's hand as they wove their way through the sea of people.

"I hate this airport," Dom grumbled as he led them all through the bustling crowds of travelers between the hellish customs lines and where drivers would be waiting to pick them up. The people in the airport seemed to sense the same authority in Dom that the athletes at OBX did, the vast majority of them giving way to his long strides and laser-like focus on getting them where they needed to be.

The click-clack of Caroline's heels followed him close behind, a similar stride, shoulders back and head held high like she owned the world or at least thought she did. Indy had barely been able to look either of them in the eye after the office incident and she wasn't sure she ever would be able to get the image of them screwing on Dom's desk out of her head. She trailed a few feet behind Caroline, feeling Jasmine at her side and Jack hovering just behind her. She always knew where he was and glancing over her shoulder, she saw Teddy bringing up the rear, practiced indifference across his face, gigantic headphones drowning out the buzz of the packed airport terminal.

There were two drivers standing with a slew of others, both holding signs that said, *Outerbanks Tennis Academy* in big bold letters.

"Mr. Kingston?" the first driver, tall, thin and balding, with wisps of red hair on the sides, asked Dom. "Is this the whole party?"

"We're all here."

"Excellent. I'll be driving Ms. Morneau and yourself to the Dorchester. Geoffrey will take the others to Mr. Russell's home."

He led them out to the curb where two sleek black Mercedes were waiting. The drivers began to load their bags into the trunks when Dom's phone started to bleep almost simultaneously with Caroline's. Indy narrowed her eyes as her coach and her agent looked at each other, a silent conversation passing between them before Dom turned to his driver. "Change of plans. Indiana will be riding with us. We'll drop her off at Alex's and then continue on to the hotel."

"What? No, it's fine," Indy said, stepping toward the other car.

"Indiana, you should come with us," Caroline said softly, then looked over her shoulder at Jack. Indy turned toward him and watched as his eyes narrowed, but he nodded slowly.

"Go with them, Indy," he whispered. "We'll all fit in the cars easier and you won't have to watch Teddy mope for another half hour."

Jasmine was already in the car and she stuck her head back out the door. "Are we going or not?"

Indy locked eyes with Dom, who held her gaze steadily, but then he looked away, a flush creeping up over his neck. How was he going to coach her when he could barely look at her? May as well try and make things a little less awkward. "Alright. See you guys in a little bit."

She slid into the back seat with Caroline while Dom sat up front with the driver and they pulled away from the curb and set off toward the M4 that would take them into London.

"Look, if this is about what happened yesterday."

Dom turned in the seat, looking back at her, "Indy, that's not something you should have had to see and we are so sorry. It's not…"

Indy just shook her head, cutting him off like he'd just done to her. "No, it's fine. I didn't tell my dad and I'm not going to, so you can both relax."

Caroline flushed a color somewhere between purple and red, exhaling through her nose, but shook her head. "This is not about us, Indiana. Do you wish to tell her, Dominic?"

"Those texts we just got, it was from the tournament director. You've been granted a wild card, Indy."

"To Eastbourne? Next week?"

"To the Championships, Indiana. To Wimbledon," Caroline said, patting her hand lightly.

"Congratulations," the driver cut in over the deafening silence.

"Thank you. Wait, are you sure?" she asked Caroline and then turned to Dom again.

"We're sure," Dom said.

"Oh my God, did you guys like call in a favor to keep me quiet? I already told you I didn't say anything to my dad. If you two want to screw each other, that's…"

Dom coughed, pounding on his own chest and Caroline's eyes widened, "Indiana!"

"What? Like it didn't cross your mind," Indy said, rolling her eyes and leaning back against the seat. "You didn't, did you?"

"No, of course not. They saw you play in Paris and they want the French Open Girls' champion in the main draw."

"This is amazing. I can't wait to tell everyone. Penny's going to freak and Jasmine, she's going to..." Indy trailed off. Jasmine probably wouldn't be all that excited about it.

"Indy, that's why we wanted you to ride with us," Dom said slowly. "Remember what we talked about in Paris, about your endurance level, about how, if you had advanced in the doubles tournament and the juniors singles that you would have a choice to make."

"Oh shit. I...I can't do both?"

"If you had a wildcard for the doubles, then maybe, but you two have to go through qualifying. You can't exhaust yourself for three days trying to get into the doubles tournament and go into your first singles match, where you'll most certainly be playing against one of the top players in the world, completely exhausted. It's counterproductive," Dom explained. "Jasmine has been around this game for a long time, Indy. She'll understand."

"She'll understand," Indy repeated, running a hand through her hair. "She'll understand that I'm dropping her and she'll hate me. I told her in Paris that I wouldn't do that."

"I can do it, if you want. Explain the situation to her, try to soften the blow a little bit."

Indy glanced out the car window just as the scenery started to change from nondescript buildings into London's outskirts, small groupings of houses and then more stately architecture. Her stomach rolled a little from being on the left side of the road, feeling like she was seconds from a head-on collision on the wrong side.

"No. I'll do it."

She could see flashes of the Thames as they edged into the city, then a sign that they were entering the Royal Borough of Kensington, the streets lined with expensive shops and elegant townhouses. There were some places in the US that tried to mimic the look that London had created over the centuries, but none of them quite measured up. Another sign declared that they'd left Kensington and had moved into the posh neighborhood of Chelsea. Then the car slowed and they turned onto a street called Egerton Crescent, white houses with black wrought iron faux balconies lined the street. A half hour before, Indy couldn't wait to arrive, to see Penny and Alex, stretch out and maybe grab something to eat with her friends in London and now she didn't even want to get out of the car, even when trapped with the two people she'd walked in on boning just the day before.

The driver didn't give her a choice. He opened the door and waited expectantly for her to get out, the others from the car ahead of them already on the sidewalk, up at Alex's home. The door flew open wide and Penny was standing there with a huge smile on her face. She practically skipped down the steps toward them, no sign of her walking boot, but no sign of her limp either.

~

"Hey girl," Penny said, pulling Indy in for a hug. Her arms smaller than her brother's but comforting in their own way. She hadn't realized just how much she'd missed her friend.

"I missed you," Indy whispered and tightened her arms around her.

Penny pulled back a little. "You okay?"

Indy sniffed and nodded. "Yeah, can we talk in a little bit though?" she said under her breath. She needed to run all this by Penny. She was the only person who'd understand this feeling, stuck between what a normal person would do for a friend and what they had to do as professionals, that the sport had to come first, even over a promise.

"Of course," she said, barely getting the words out before Jack came barreling across the sidewalk and lifted Penny up into a bear hug.

"Heard you were practicing," he said, setting her down gently.

"Save the lecture for later, bro," Teddy said, pushing Jack out of the way and hugging his twin sister.

Jasmine stepped up to the group and Indy met her eye. They were both only children, just one of the many things they realized they had in common after they got over hating each other.

"Hey Jas," Penny said, once Teddy let her go. Jasmine smiled. "Come on in everyone. Alex and Paolo have a practice session, but they'll be back soon."

Dom and Caroline hovered in the background for a second and Penny tilted her head. "Are you guys coming in?"

Dom shook his head. "No, we're going to head over and check into the hotel."

"Yes, put our bags down, get settled," Caroline finished for him.

Indy scoffed, and Dom shifted back and forth on his feet. Could they be any more obvious?

The cars pulled away and Penny led them up the stairs into the townhouse. The front hall had a vaulted ceiling, a small iron chandelier hanging down and a wood floor polished to a high sheen, their reflections only blurred a little in the chestnut stain, the walls covered in a white glossy wainscoting. Indy had a strange feeling wash over her seeing Penny in Alex's house. It almost felt like she belonged there.

Teddy didn't even look around, he just turned to Penny. "Where can I put my shit?"

Penny snorted. "Nice to see you too, Teddy," she said. "Come on, your rooms are upstairs."

She led Jack and Teddy to the first room at the top of the long stairwell and they disappeared into it, letting their suitcases drop by the door and falling into the two full beds in the guest room. She then motioned for Indy and Jasmine to follow her further down the hallway. "This is you guys. I'm sorry you have to share."

"No problem, this is a lot better than a hotel," Jasmine said, flopping back onto the first of two beds, covered in white fluffy comforters with large pillows at the head.

Indy stepped over the wood floors and onto the ivory colored area rug at the center of the room then over to the bed on the opposite wall. Would Jasmine still feel that way after she told her what was going to happen in the next two weeks or rather what *wasn't* going to happen? That their journey toward the main doubles draw at Wimbledon was over before it really began.

"Don't fall asleep," Penny warned. "We have reservations in a couple of hours for dinner and if you go to sleep now you'll screw your sleep pattern up for the entire time you're here."

Jasmine groaned and yanked her suitcase upright, unzipping and digging through it, finding a change of clothes and her bath things right at the top. "Alright, I call first shower. Where's the bathroom?"

Penny pointed out the door. "Second door on the left."

Indy waited until she heard the bathroom door shut, the sound of the bathroom fan click on and then the water running before she turned to Penny who'd waited patiently, sitting down at a white dressing table chair.

"I got a singles wildcard to Wimbledon," she said quietly.

"Oh my God, Indy. That's amazing. I don't know why it took them so long, but of course, you should be playing. The draw's not out for a few days still, but...oh."

"Yeah, *oh*. Jasmine's going to freak. Dom and Caroline were adamant about it. There's no way I can do doubles quals and prepare for the singles tournament."

"You're going to tell her tonight?"

"I have to. If I wait any longer, it'll be like lying." A little voice in the back of her mind started to shout that she was keeping something from Penny as well, something huge, but it didn't feel like the right moment. Penny always put tennis first, she'd understand. Besides, she and Jack agreed that they'd tell her together and right now he was probably in the shower, getting ready for their night out. Her mind drifted for a second, imagining rivulets of water sluicing over lean, tanned muscle, getting caught in dark curly chest hair but she blinked the fantasy away, focusing on Penny.

"Makes sense," Penny said. "I know I'd want to be told right away. Just..."

"What?"

"Just don't let this bring you down completely, okay? I know you guys just got on good terms, but you got a wildcard to *Wimbledon*, Indy. That's huge. You get the right draw, beat the right people, it could make your career. Forget about winning the junior tournament, you could be on tour almost full time. Some hurt feelings now are totally worth it."

"Are they?"

Penny shrugged. "For me it would be, but I'm not you."

"No, you're not. Ugh. This is gonna suck."

"What's gonna suck?" Jasmine asked, walking through the door in white shorts and a bright pink long-sleeved see-through top over a cami, a towel wrapped around her head to keep her wet hair off the pretty shirt.

Penny stood, looking back and forth between them before tilting her head toward Indy in a silent question. Should I stay? Indy shook her head just once and Penny's eyes flashed back to Jasmine for a brief moment before she said, "I'm just...I'm gonna go get ready."

"What's gonna suck?" Jasmine repeated.

"Why Dom and Caroline made me ride with them over here. They had some news."

"Bad news? Is everything okay?"

The concern in her voice made Indy's stomach twist. A lump formed in her throat she felt the muscles in her legs and arms start to tighten. It was just like she used to feel before a big match, before Jasmine had come along and talked her through those issues and now she had to tell her that she was dropping her. She took a deep breath and swallowed back the nerves. "Good news, mostly, but…" she trailed off. It was better to just put it out there, rip off the bandage.

Chapter 11

June 19th

"Okay," Jasmine said, shrugging her shoulder and laying her toiletry bag on the nightstand beside the bed she'd claimed.

"Okay?" Indy repeated.

"What else do you want me to say? You have to do what you have to do, Indy. You're right, it sucks and I'm kind of annoyed that you talked to Penny about it before me, you know, your partner. But I can't ask you to pass up a chance to play in the main draw for doubles qualifications. That would be pretty self-centered of me." She tried to keep the bite out of her voice, but some of it seeped through and she knew Indy could tell by the way her mouth twisted into a small pout. "It's annoying that I'm here so early. I could have stayed back at OBX and practiced with Amy to keep my singles game sharp. It's two weeks until the junior tournament starts."

Indy nodded. "Right, you could have practiced with Amy. Jesus, Jasmine, if you're pissed off, just admit it."

"I'm not." She really wasn't. She was hurt and that was stupid because Indy's choice was the right one. Still, they'd been working toward Wimbledon together and now that was shot to hell. "I'm not pissed off."

"I'm sorry I told Penny first, but I had to be sure I was doing the right thing."

Jasmine scoffed. "Tennis comes first for Penny. Wrong person to go to if you're debating tennis versus anything else in life."

"Yeah, I guess so," Indy said and then moved to her suitcase, digging through the clothes and pulling out some crumpled fabric and a small toiletry bag. "I'm going to shower."

She left the room and Jasmine sank back onto her bed and blew out a breath. Penny and Indy had understated it. Sucks didn't even come close to describing this clusterfuck. Doubles was her way in to the pro ranks, the thing that would keep her afloat until she could make a name for herself as a singles player. Maybe her parents and Felix Wolner and Dom and everyone else were right. Maybe she should just go play in college and stop deluding herself. Then, in a few years, maybe she could go pro and see where it led. What else was she supposed to do? Just be left behind in everyone's dust as they went on to fame and fortune?

Jasmine yanked the towel off her head, letting her hair fall down around her shoulders. She stood and strode across the room, staring at her reflection in the mirror hanging on the wall above the dresser. The long dark locks were still damp and she needed a blow dryer if she was going to be ready on time. Digging through her bag, she found one quickly, but came up empty looking for the outlet adapter, the only thing between a working blow dryer and blowing every fuse in Alex Russell's house. "Crap."

Penny probably had one, she thought, as she left the room and headed down the hallway toward what she guessed was Alex's bedroom. The door was shut now though and she could hear muffled voices, one much deeper than the other from behind the solid wood barrier. Not a chance in hell she was going to interrupt whatever was going on in there. She spun around and headed toward the guys' room, but instead, collided with a warm body behind her and a hand shot out to steady her at the elbow.

"Jasmine Randazzo," the voice belonging to the body said, the soft accent rolling the double z at the end of her last name in the way only an Italian would.

"Sorry," she said, looking up into the crystal clear blue eyes of Paolo Macchia, crinkled at the sides as a smile widened over his face.

"Figurati," he said and when he noticed she had no idea what he was saying, he translated. "Don't worry about it." His warm hand squeezed her elbow and then he stepped back a little. "Do you remember, we met in Paris?"

"Paolo, right?" she asked, playing it cool. Of course she remembered. Who could forget him, with his olive skin and dark curls and a body like *that?*

He nodded and then glanced over her shoulder. "Were you looking for Penny?"

"Yeah," she said, but laughed a little. "I think she's a little busy."

"They are almost always *busy.*"

Jasmine groaned.

"Exactly."

She laughed and shook her head. "You don't have a blow dryer, do you?"

"Blow-dryer?" His forehead crinkled.

"Hair dryer? Secadora de pelo?" She tried in Spanish as well.

"Asciugacapelli," he translated and nodded, motioning for her to follow him down the hallway. His room was right next to Jack's and Teddy's and she leaned on the frame of his doorway while he unplugged his *asciugacapelli* from the wall. "All yours."

He held it out to her and she took it, letting her fingertips brush against his deliberately. He chuckled softly and held the contact for a moment, before she chickened out a little and took it from him.

She turned to go back to her room just as Jack and Teddy emerged from theirs, both in dress pants and collared shirts. Teddy in gray and Jack in a violet color, both Harrison brothers looked like they stepped off the pages of a J Crew catalogue.

As far as she knew, Paolo had never met either of them. "Paolo, this is Jack and Teddy Harrison. Penny's brothers."

"She's told me much about you both," Paolo said, shaking both their hands firmly.

"Paolo was just lending me his asciugacapelli," she said the word slowly, but he hummed his approval at her pronunciation.

"His what?" Teddy asked, his eyes flying back and forth between her and Paolo, his eyes finally staying on her for what felt like the first time in forever.

"His hairdryer, little brother," Jack said, clapping him on the shoulder and nodding at the object in her hands.

"Oh, right." He looked away again, even as Jasmine tried to meet his eye.

"Are we having a hallway party?" Indy's voice rang out from the other end of the hall.

"Something like that," Jack called back. "Come on boys, let's let the ladies finish getting ready. On my way in, I thought I saw a nice bottle of bourbon that any man dating my sister would be wise to let me sample."

The guys all headed down together and Jasmine turned, hairdryer in hand, forcing a half smile in Indy's direction.

~

They dressed in silence, moving around the room, keeping a heavy distance between each other as they dried hair and applied makeup. Jasmine wasn't going to break the silence. She'd been honest with Indy, she wasn't angry, but this tension wasn't her fault either. If Indy wanted things to be less awkward, she was going to have to make the first move.

A half hour of silence and Penny showed up at their door. "Are you guys ready?" she asked, wearing a pale pink slip dressed with lace at the hem falling to her mid-thigh, gold heels making her nearly Indy's height.

"Ladies," Alex said from over her shoulder. "You both look lovely."

Paolo, Jack and Teddy were all in the library sipping what Jasmine recognized as ridiculously expensive alcohol that her dad was particularly fond of.

"We got a head start," Paolo said before he gulped down the last of the amber liquid in his tumbler. The other guys followed suit. Jasmine hadn't had a sip of alcohol since France and when

Paolo refilled his glass, she stepped up and took it from him, downing it in one gulp, licking her lips.

"Good," she managed, her voice a little raspy, and he took the glass back, as Alex announced that the cars had arrived.

The restaurant was a London hotspot and, as usual, when you were with Penny and Alex, the sidewalk was lined with photographers all wanting to get a good shot of the celebrity golden couple.

Jasmine stepped out of the car, her heel catching immediately in a crevice between the cobblestones that lined the old London street, but a warm hand at her back, the same hand that steadied her earlier in the hallway, caught her and kept her balanced.

"Thank you," she said and as they made their way as a group through the throng of photographers, Paolo stayed with her, his hand at the small of her back, spreading warmth over her skin like nothing had in a very long time.

The maître de took one look at their party and led them to one of the best tables in the house. It was the kind of quality place that kept their best tables out of the center of the restaurant, allowing celebrity clientele a modicum of privacy rather than using the cache to attract other patrons. Their table was up a flight of stairs, overlooking the rest of the restaurant, big enough for them all to sit comfortably, but not too large to have a conversation across it. The walls were lined with dark wood paneling, the sconces lit dimly, creating an atmosphere just a little bit romantic, if you wanted it to be. As Paolo waved away their host and pulled out her chair for her, allowing her to sit before he sat down beside her, Jasmine realized that she definitely wanted it to be.

Before she could blink, a glass of white wine was put in front of her and appetizers started to flow out of the kitchen at an alarming rate. Apparently, the chef was a friend of Alex's and had decided to send them a little bit of everything on the menu and some things that weren't.

"Where are you from, exactly?" Jasmine asked. Paolo had to lean down a little to hear her or maybe he just wanted to be closer. She preferred the latter.

"Milan," Paolo said. "Randazzo, that's an Italian name." He left the question unasked.

"My dad's family is from a small village just north of Trieste originally. They came over to escape Mussolini."

"My family has been in Milan for hundreds of years, maybe thousands. I left when I was a boy to study at the tennis academy in France."

"That must have been difficult," she said.

He nodded, taking another sip of wine. "You were lucky that your parents had their school. Alex has said it is an excellent facility and while perhaps he was a little biased by the company he found there, he would not praise it if he didn't think it worthy."

"It's home," she said simply.

Paolo smiled at her. "Perhaps one day, I will come and train with you all."

"I think I'd like that."

He leaned in a little closer so that his mouth was nearly against her ear. "Am I..?" he began, but then started over. "I don't mean to over step, but that younger Harrison brother, he has been giving us the evil eye since we sat down."

Jasmine chanced a look over the white of the tablecloth and saw Teddy staring at them, not exactly frowning. She recognized the expression. It's the same one he'd worn when Amy arrived at OBX last week. She didn't know what was going through his head, but he clearly wasn't happy. Maybe he should have thought about that before he decided to screw the girl who broke his heart.

"He's my friend," she said. "Nothing else." For the first time, maybe ever, the words felt like the truth. She meant it. Teddy was her friend and that was it. He made it clear that it wasn't in the cards and if he wanted to glare over the table at a hot guy showing interest in her, that was his problem, not hers.

"Then that sad look on your face earlier. That was not for him?"

He'd been able to tell she was upset? Was she that transparent? "No, I got some," she hesitated, choosing her words carefully, "disappointing news. Nothing at all to do with Teddy or anyone else." Teddy would actually have to be speaking to her to upset her.

"So there is no one else?"

"No, there's no one."

"Ah, that is very good news. Now I shall make it my mission to distract you from this disappointing news you received," Paolo said, taking her hand up and pressing a kiss to it. Jasmine looked around quickly and most of the table had seen it, but Jack cleared his throat and kept up his conversation, drawing everyone's eyes away, except Teddy's. She could still feel his gaze on them, but instead, she turned in her chair a little, crossing her legs and shifting closer to Paolo.

"Distract away."

~

They stayed at the restaurant as it swelled with patrons until almost everyone else had cleared out, waiters had kept the food and wine flowing, though the guys packed it away, the girls had to look on in envy. There was something a little unfair about the male metabolism, but regardless, Jasmine sat back in her chair and sighed, more than happy with the pasta primavera she'd gobbled down.

"A girl who can eat," Paolo said, a hand rubbing over his stomach.

"That's what gets you?"

"Every time."

To her left, Penny pushed back out of her chair and signaled to her with a toss of her head. She looked toward Indy, but she was in the middle of a heated debate with Alex about soccer, apparently their loyalties in conflict. "Be right back," she said and stood up, following Penny down a hallway toward the ladies room.

"Indy told me about having to withdraw from doubles."

Jasmine shrugged. "She has to do what's right for her." The wine had dulled the pain of that particular truth.

"She does," Penny agreed. "Do you still want to play doubles?"

"Why, do you want to play?"

Penny scoffed.

"So, if not you?"

"Natalie Grogan."

The girl she'd lost to in the French Open juniors, a sixteen-year-old up and comer who'd be sure to leap at the chance to qualify for the women's double's tournament.

"You're sure you can make that happen?"

"Pretty sure."

"Because if she turns me down, that's worse than not asking at all."

Penny looked her right in the eye and nodded. "She won't turn you down."

"Why not?"

"Because I'm the one who's going to ask her," she said, pulling her phone out of her bag and tapping away at it for a moment. "All I need is for you to give me the okay."

Jasmine chewed at the inside of her cheek for a minute. What did she have to lose? Natalie was a really good player; she'd seen that first hand in France. "Okay."

Penny pressed send.

Jasmine followed her back to the table and saw Paolo had been pulled into the debate over the Champions League final just a few weeks ago. She sat down and leaned forward into the conversation. "Barca should have been in the final. That penalty kick against Man United was bullshit."

"Ah. She knows football," Paolo said, slinging an arm around, his thumb stroking lightly at the skin of her shoulder, "I am in love."

Jasmine shivered and ignored the glare she could feel from the opposite side of the table. If Teddy had a problem, he was going to have to suck it up. She felt another set of eyes on her and Jasmine turned to her left. Penny just nodded once. Teddy didn't want her and apparently neither did Indy, but there were other guys and other doubles partners and she was going to be just fine.

Chapter 12

June 20th

Penny leaned back on the trainer's table and rotated her foot, the trainer on a stool awaiting her judgment. Just enough range of motion to play, not enough to let her ankle roll. Perfect. She nodded her approval.

"Take it easy today. There was a little more swelling than I'd like to see this morning," the trainer cautioned and she nodded. There was more swelling than she'd like to see too, especially just two days from the start of the Championships. Just a short drive outside of London, twenty minutes from Alex's house, the grounds at Wimbledon were ready for the most important two weeks of tennis all year. Lush green courts, white lines painted perfectly. The strawberries and Pimms on ice waiting for the crowds to arrive. Of all the majors, it had the most history and with it, the most prestige. Winning Wimbledon, for most tennis players, Penny included, was the goal from the moment they picked up a racket.

"Got it," she said, and hopped down from the table and then bounced up and down to make sure she had enough give in the wrap.

The trainer gave a long-suffering sigh, the sigh of a man who'd had athletes ignore him every day of his career.

Indy popped her head into the room. "You good to go?"

"Yeah, let's get out there."

They'd taken the drive up to Wimbledon early that morning to get in an early practice session and if they weren't too beat, to catch Jasmine's qualification match. Things had been awkward in the house since Indy broke the news and Penny couldn't imagine how thick the air was behind the door to their bedroom. It was why she'd never really mixed tennis and friendship. It was tough to be friends when your choices could make or break someone else's career.

The practice courts were lined with reporters, as usual, and some of the club members had been allowed in to observe the sessions. Word spread quickly that Penny would be on the court truly testing her ankle for the first time since

France. She and Indy would be playing a mock set, both of them not having played a real game for weeks and with the tournament only a few days away, it was time to see how it would feel while playing full out.

Dom was waiting for them on the court. "You ladies stretched and ready to go?"

"All set," Indy said, swinging her arm around in circles.

Penny stretched her neck back and forth before rolling her shoulders. "Let's go."

After warmups, a few groundstrokes each and some serves, Penny chucked a ball to Indy and yelled, "Bring it all out." Indy's serve was one of the best in the game, the sole reason she'd been able to take a year off of tennis and still rise like mercury through the junior ranks, but Penny's return game was the best in the world.

"You sure you're ready for this?" Indy asked.

"Shut up and serve, Gaffney."

The first was a rocket down the center line and Penny got a racket on it, not a full swing, but a block back deep and beyond the baseline. Her eye twitched a little, checking the strings on her racket, spacing them out as she moved to the other side of the court.

"15-Love," Dom yelled helpfully from the sidelines. Indy snorted and Penny rolled her eyes. The last time they played, way back when she first arrived at OBX, Indy hadn't even been able to secure a point against her. That streak was over now.

Indy served hard and flat, into the body. Penny let her body just react, a full swing this time, but she sent it soaring out past the line again.

"30-love," Dom said.

Crossing back to the other side, Penny frowned. She wasn't reacting fast enough. Bouncing on the balls of her feet, she glanced down at her ankle, which gave a little twinge in response. She was rusty, but she didn't have time for that. It was time to get her ass in gear.

Two more serves and two more crappy returns and Penny could feel the tension start to pinch at her neck. Too much time off the court had made her just a fraction slower. On the clay of Roland Garros, she would have been able to absorb it, but on grass where the ball would fly fast and true, it would be a major liability. She'd have to make up for it on her own serves. Keep the games short and sweet; no breaks of serve and no long rallies.

Easier said than done against the best players in the world.

An hour later, grass stains on the white practice gear she'd been given from Nike, she and Indy were knotted at six games apiece and Dom was waving them in from the sidelines. "That's enough, ladies. You've already put in more than I wanted you to."

Relief coursed through her, something Penny had never felt at the end of a practice session before, at least not in a very, very long time. Indy had put up one hell of a fight and her ankle was throbbing. Not the sharp pain of a tear, but a burn through the entire joint, the tendon pulsing, making her skin swell against the wrap.

"You want to go check out Jasmine's match?" Indy asked. "And I'm not going to lie, I'm kind of hoping you say no."

"We should go," Penny said. It would be a nice distraction from the pain. "It would look weird if we didn't."

"I am weird. Everyone knows that already."

"Yes, but you don't want things to look suspicious, like you're fighting or something. People would talk. Besides, Natalie is one of your main competitors for the junior title. It'll be a good opportunity to scout her."

"People friggin' talk anyway," Indy muttered and Penny couldn't help but agree. "And I don't plan on having to play the juniors. If I make it past the first week, I'll have to drop out."

The odds that Indy would make it past the first week were pretty slim. Though the draw hadn't been released yet, as a wildcard entry, she'd be facing a really tough opponent, someone in the top ten at least. Penny opened her mouth to respond, but then thought better of it. Sometimes, it was better to learn things like that from experience. She saw Dom in the distance, waving her down the hallway toward the press conference room. "I've gotta do this presser. I'll meet you there, okay?"

Indy laughed. "You're making me go and you're abandoning me. Some friend."

"God, stop being dramatic. She's your friend; you should want to watch her match," Penny snapped and flinched, immediately regretting it. "Sorry. I'm…"

"You're annoyed that I might have beaten you if Dom hadn't stopped us just now," Indy finished for her.

Blinking at the other girl, she shook her head. That hadn't even entered into her mind. It was her ankle; she could practically see it, red, maybe purple and swollen, needing some time in an ice bucket before she'd be able to walk on it later. "No, not at all," she said. "Where did that come from?"

"It's okay. It's written all over your face," Indy said with a little laugh. "You make this scrunched up, totally unimpressed face when you're upset."

"I'm upset that my ankle hurts. You played well."

Indy bit her lip. "Sorry, me and my big mouth."

"You really should have a lock on that thing. I'll see you after, okay?"

"Yeah, alright."

Penny shook her head as Indy turned into the player's dressing room and she continued on down the hallway toward her coach, handing her bag off.

"Ready?" he asked, eyes narrowing in concern that she put most of her weight on her good ankle.

"To face those vultures? As I'll ever be."

"You alright?"

"Fine. Let's just get this over with."

She walked out onto the tiny stage, reporters packing the room and the cameras in the back were rolling.

"Hey guys," she said, getting comfortable in her chair.

"Penny," Harold Hodges began, "how's your ankle?"

"Doing fine. Pushed it hard today, so I'll see how it feels tomorrow, but so far so good."

"Is 'fine' enough to make it through the fortnight?" a British reporter she didn't recognize asked?

"It'll have to be."

A reporter from the back of the room stood up, "Penny, we did some calculations and if you win this tournament and Zina Lutrova loses in the quarters, you will be the new number one. What does that mean to you?"

"Being number one in the world would be a huge accomplishment, but I'm not here to worry about that. I'm here to win Wimbledon."

"And if the ankle doesn't hold up?"

"It's going to have to, isn't it?"

"If it doesn't?"

"It will."

~

The same trainer who wrapped her ankle was the one who unwrapped it and he shook his head as he pulled the tape free. "You are going to do some damage to yourself, young lady," he lectured, but nodded to the ice bucket.

Penny slid the injured foot into the freezing water and hissed, a thousand tiny needles stabbing at the injury all at once. "It'll be fine."

"That's what they all say."

He left the room and Penny sat back against the wall, letting her eyes drift shut. She heard the creak of the door opening and closing again and then Dom's voice. "How does it feel?"

"Hurts," she said and pulled it out to show him. The cold water had made the swelling go down a little bit.

"Maybe we should withdraw."

Penny sniffed, still not opening her eyes. "That's not an option."

"Did you see how you played out there today? Indy's good, Pen, but she's not that good, not yet."

She waved a hand in the air and put her foot back into the icy water. "Rust."

"Open your damn eyes when you talk to me," he snapped. Dom had never spoken to her like that, not on his worst day. Her eyes flew open. He was leaning against the opposite wall, arms crossed over his chest and his mouth was set in a thin line. "It wasn't rust. It was pain."

"No it wasn't. I could barely feel it."

"Because you have the pain threshold of a gladiator. I know what I saw. You were hesitating. Your footwork was slow and you instinctively went for shots that would put less impact on that ankle."

She shrugged. "So I focus more on playing my game. It'll be fine."

"It might not be and what if you hurt it worse? There are other tournaments, Penny."

"It's Wimbledon. I'm not withdrawing. I played on it in France and it was fine."

"You played on it in France for a few minutes. You were out there for an hour today and look at it."

"I'm not withdrawing," she said through clenched teeth.

Dom pushed off the wall, throwing his hands in the air. "You ever see the video of my last match?" She had. It was at the U.S. Open, against a sixteen year old Alex Russell. Dom's knee had given out and he was helped off the court by the trainers at the end of the match. "I don't want that for you, Pen."

"You had nearly ten years on tour on that knee, Dom. I have an ankle strain. It's not the same thing," she said, quietly. He rarely talked about his own career and it made her realize just how much he wanted her to withdraw. "I'm not you."

"No, you're not. You have ten times the talent I ever had and up until now, I thought you were about a hundred times smarter."

Penny sighed and lifted her foot from the bucket. Enough time had passed for the ice to do its job. "Dom, I know my limits. If it's too much, I'll withdraw. I promise." There was no chance in hell that was happening, but at least it would shut him up.

Her phone buzzed with a text from Indy. *You coming?* Thumb flying over the screen, she texted back, *in a bit.*

"I've got to get back to Jasmine's match," Dom said. "See you there?"

"Yeah, I've just got to shower."

~

By the time she made it out to the qualification courts, the match was nearly over. Dom was still there, but Indy was long gone. Penny caught sight of Paolo Macchia near the edge of the crowd, hat and sunglasses firmly in place to keep a low profile. She was sporting a similar look. "How're they doing?" she asked at a whisper.

"6-2, 4-1. They'll move on easily," he said, his eyes not leaving the court for a second. "Indy went back to the house."

Penny twisted her mouth into a pout. She didn't really want to stand around on her ankle waiting for the match to be over. "I'm going to call a car then. You want to come with me?"

"No," he said, and she smiled at him and patted him on the back. He was going to need a lot of luck if he wanted Jasmine. Penny couldn't remember a time when the other girl wasn't in love with Teddy.

"Okay, see you later."

"Ciao."

A car was brought around quickly. "Miss Harrison, where to?" the driver asked.

"Number 60 Egerton Crescent."

"Ah, you're staying with our boy then? Good, good. You two make a lovely couple, miss."

"Thank you," she said, for a moment, her mind drifting away from her damned ankle and back to Alex.

"Be nice if you both could win it this year. Decided to adopt you as an honorary Brit. Closest thing we have on the women's side, innit?"

She laughed. "I guess so."

It took a little longer to get back home than it had on the way there. The morning rush hour was just starting to build, but even still, it wouldn't take long for the green of the suburbs to turn into the row houses of Chelsea. "Now, you rest that ankle of yours, miss. Gotta have you nice and healthy on the day." She nearly snapped at him. She'd opened her mouth to tell him that her ankle was fine, and that she didn't need to rest it or anything like that, she just needed people to shut the hell up about it and let her play, but then she caught his eye in the rearview mirror and he was smiling broadly at her, white teeth stark against his dark complexion. She couldn't let her frustration get to her, couldn't let it dictate everything, on the court or off it.

"Thank you…" she trailed off.

"Ahmed."

"Thanks, Ahmed," she said, making a mental note to request him as a driver for the tournament and settling in for the twenty-minute ride back to Alex's house, where he'd likely still be lounging in bed and she could crawl back in next to him and let everything else slip away.

Chapter 13

June 20th

Indy wrung her fingers together, pacing the upstairs hallway of Alex's Russell's home. She'd ducked out of Jasmine's match a little early, despite what Penny said about needing to show unity. Jasmine and Natalie had it under control and her presence didn't have anything to do with it. Jasmine wasn't going to miss her, that's for sure. Her doubles partner, or former doubles partner, had barely spoken a word to her since she broke the news but still insisted to everyone else that she wasn't angry. Penny had found the perfect solution for her, but if anything, that made it worse, the tennis world speculating about why they'd split up after doing so well together at the French Open. She just wanted to get away from it all, but now that she was back in the relative privacy of Alex's house, Penny and Paolo still at the All England Club, the only thing she could think about was tiptoeing into Jack's room, crawling into his bed and just…she didn't know what. Her mind sped from curling up in a ball next to him and falling asleep to every other far-less innocent option under the sun. They hadn't had a real chance to be alone in nearly a week and it was wearing on her. She didn't realize how much she'd come to depend on their stolen moments together in France and back at OBX.

Finally pushing down the butterflies in her stomach, she took a deep breath and opened his door. There was nothing to be nervous about. Not really.

The room was still dark, curtains drawn closed. Teddy's bed was rumpled and slept in, the dark comforter in a lump at the center of the mattress. Jack was asleep on his stomach in his bed, the covers shoved down at his waist, the muscles in his back rippling as he shifted in his sleep. One arm was shoved up under his pillow, holding onto it for dear life, the other tossed carelessly out to the side. Indy slipped off her shoes and then her socks, kneeling gingerly on the mattress, trying not to disturb him at first. She lifted a leg over his body, settling herself slowly onto his lower back. He grunted but didn't stir.

Slowly, she slid her hands up over his back, then brought them down again, letting her nails scratch lightly on his skin. Again, she repeated the motion with a little more pressure, before kneading the palms of her hands against his shoulders, massaging the muscles. He tensed beneath her and then, with a groan, relaxed into her touch.

"I'll give you a half hour to stop that," he mumbled into the pillow and then groaned again when she hit a particularly tense spot. "Jesus, you've got strong hands."

"Just what every girl wants to hear. Such a sweet talker, Jack," she said, leaning down and pressing a kiss to his shoulder blade.

He pushed up off the mattress and she moved up onto her knees to give him room. Settling back down, he took her hips in his hands and drew her against him. "You want sweet talk?"

"Mmmm," she said, sliding down against him harder and rolling her hips a little, but his hands, tightening against her waist, stopped the motion. Then, before she could respond, he'd rolled them over, pressing her full body into the mattress.

'No, I don't think you do," he muttered. "Sweet talk isn't what does it for you, Indiana."

Indy raised her eyebrows. Where was he going with this? "No?"

"Nope," he said, leaning over and putting his mouth, hot and open, against that spot just below her ear. "You see, I've noticed something."

"What's that?" she breathed, her body arching into his; but he held her down.

"I've noticed that you like when I kiss you here," he said, brushing his lips against her skin, "but you love it when I..." he trailed off, scraping his teeth along the same spot, making her whole body jolt. "And," he began again, "I've noticed that you like my hands in your hair." He cupped the back of her head, freeing her ponytail free; she nodded. "But you love it when," he trailed off again, tugging sharply at the locks of hair in his fist. Indy groaned and threw her head back at the sensation. "So, no Indiana, I don't think you want sweet talk. In fact, I'm pretty sure you want the opposite."

How had he known that about her? She hadn't even know it herself, not really. She'd had a few boyfriends, but none of them had made her feel like this and most of the physical stuff had consisted of heavy, unpracticed hands groping at her. This was different. Every touch was purposeful, every little bit of contact, soft or not, meant to bring her pleasure. Her mind reeled when his mouth collided with hers, his tongue pushing past her lips. It was a little sloppy and pretty damn rough and she friggin' loved it.

"Am I right?" he asked, tearing himself away and grinning down at her, but her hands slid up into his hair, digging her nails into his scalp and pulling him back down. His hips thrust against her and his eyes slipped shut.

"Seems like you're not one for sweet either," she mumbled against his mouth.

"Never said I was. Why do you think I want you? Wild's more my style, Indiana. Always has been." He said the words as he dragged his mouth away from hers, trailing a path over her jaw line and down to her neck, using his teeth again, this time against her pulse point. Indy pushed up against him, bringing her legs around his waist, pulling him in as close as she could. His hands slid along her sides, pushing the material of her t-shirt out of the way. Her hands twisted into the elastic of the boxer briefs he slept in, before a wicked eye flashed through her head. She pulled the elastic away and then let it snap back into place with a satisfying thwap against his hip. Jack chuckled, a deep, husky sound from the back of his throat. "You learn fast."

"Good teacher," she said, sitting up and letting him drag her shirt over her head, her hair falling in waves around her shoulders, so long that it covered most of the skin he'd just revealed.

He tossed the piece of cotton away and his hands cupped her face, suddenly gentle where they'd been playing rough just moments before. "You know how beautiful you are?" he whispered, leaning in slowly and sealing his lips over hers, not giving her time to answer. The kiss was gentle too. No tongues and teeth, just their mouths pressing together.

Indy pulled away, eyes closed, breath ragged, holding on to both his wrists like they were keeping her afloat. "Jack, I…"

"Hey Jack, do you want to grab some breakfast with me and Pen?"

Indy closed her eyes, knowing that voice immediately. Alex Russell was leaning on the open doorframe, arms crossed over his chest. He looked like he'd just rolled out of bed, t-shirt rumpled, basketball shorts slung low and hair in complete disarray, but his eyes were sharp enough.

"Alex?"

"Shit," Indy breathed, her forehead slamming against Jack's shoulder. That was Penny, appearing in the doorway a second later. Indy could feel her eyes on them, taking in the scene, her shirtless in her best friend's brother's bed, but she didn't look up.

"Oh my God."

"Pen," Jack started. "Let us explain."

"No," Indy said. "This is me."

"Indiana."

"Come on, love, let's let them get dressed," Alex said and she heard their footsteps headed down the stairs.

Indy slid out of bed and found her shirt where Jack had tossed it close to the doorway.

"Let me talk to my sister," Jack said, finding some cargo shorts and a t-shirt in his suitcase.

"You're her brother, Jack. She's not mad at you. She's mad at me."

"We don't know that she's mad at all," he said, but Indy spun and stared at him. "Okay, she's mad, but only because we didn't tell her and we agreed we'd tell her here…."

"Which means we kept it from her for weeks. Trust me. This is a girl thing. Let me talk to her."

~

She found Penny downstairs in the kitchen, cutting up some fruit. Indy hadn't pegged her for dramatic, but judging by the size of the knife the girl was using to chop strawberries, she was trying to make a point. She sat down on one of the cushioned stools at the island and waited. Penny just kept on chopping until a small bowl was full. Then she set the knife down on the island and looked up at her.

"How long?"

"Since we…"

Penny cut her off. "How long since you realized you liked my brother and you decided not to tell me?"

"I didn't decide not to tell you, exactly." Penny snuffed in disbelief. "Really. I mean, at first, I didn't think anything was going to happen, like I didn't have a chance in hell, so I didn't think there was a point in telling you. And then I realized he liked me back, but he was so against it, it just wasn't going to happen."

"Clearly it did."

Indy nodded.

"And when it did, you just thought, oh, I think I'll keep this from my friend. She wouldn't want to know I was fucking her brother."

"We're not…"

"Whatever. You know what I mean."

"There wasn't any time. It happened in France and you were dealing with your ankle and then you were in London and we were back home and we wanted to tell you in person."

"And once you got here, what? You changed you mind?"

"No, we just hadn't gotten the chance. I'm sorry. Jack is…he's so great and I really…"

"I know how great my brother is, Indy. Does anyone else know?"

"Jasmine knows and Caroline, but we didn't exactly tell either of them, they just found out."

"I just don't understand why you'd keep it from me. He's my brother and you're my friend. Did you think I wouldn't be happy for you guys?"

"Maybe," Indy said, shrugging. "I don't know. We didn't set out to keep it from you. It just sort of happened that way. I didn't really give it much thought, to be honest."

Penny nodded, inhaling quickly through her nose and then blowing an exhale out of her mouth. "Right. Okay." She picked up the bowl of strawberries and started to leave the room.

"Wait," Indy said, standing up and starting to follow her. "Are we okay?"

Penny turned back to her, mouth in a firm line, her eyes looking over Indy's shoulder. "I don't know."

"Do you think we will be?"

"I don't know." Penny actually looked a little sorry as she said it, her face softening for a moment, before she shook her head and swept out of the room. Watching her friend's retreating back made Indy's throat tight and her vision started to swim. A lump grew in her throat, choking her, making it impossible to fight the tears and they slipped out of the corners of her eyes, but she gasped for breath and wiped them away quickly. Crying wasn't going to make it better, the only problem was that she had no idea what would.

~

Indy sat cross-legged on Jack's bed, just staring at her hands. She didn't know what to say to Jack as he came in from talking to his sister.

"She's pissed," Jack muttered, closing the door behind him.

A harsh buzzing cut through the air and they both glared at his nightstand where his phone was lit up like a Christmas tree. He huffed out a breath. "Damn it. I'm sorry. I have to take this."

He stood up quickly and grabbed the phone.

"Who is it?"

"Sam Grogan."

"Natalie's dad/coach/manager?"

"The one and only," he said, glancing at the phone and shaking his head. He leaned over and pressed a hard kiss to her lips and then pulled away just as quickly. He stepped away and answered the call. "Jack Harrison. Yes, Mr. Grogan...of course...yes of course, but...I assure you that...right...of course you do...what's best for Natalie, of course. Well, thank you for calling and best of luck to Natalie at the Championships."

Indy sat up, biting her lip. "Not good news."

"They decided to go with another agent."

"That sucks. I'm sorry."

Jack shook his head, sitting down at the edge of the bed. "It's not just that," he said. "It's more the reason why they decided on another agent."

"Why's that?"

"Apparently, someone told him that you and I were...together."

Indy's mouth dropped open. There were only two people in the world who knew she and Jack were together, well four now, but Alex didn't care and Penny wouldn't have...would she?

"Did he keep it to himself or..." she trailed off as her phone started blinging wildly from somewhere in the sheets. It must have fallen out of her pocket when he pulled her into bed with him. She dug around for a moment and found it, glancing at the screen before tossing it aside again. The phone continued to light up, as notification after notification asking her if it was true, tagging her in posts, old "friends" suddenly checking in after months of silence, just a barrage of messages.

"It's all over the place by now." Jack pulled back and grabbed the phone, handing it to her. "Shut it off."

"Who do you think it was?" she asked, as his hands rubbed up and down her arms, thumb landing lightly on the inside of her elbow, stroking back and forth. Usually, his touch made her shiver, but now it was simply a warm, solid comfort.

"Our list of suspects is pretty short. Natalie signed with Caroline this morning, so my money is on her. Though she could have let it slip to any of the other agents who were vying to sign her. Classic maneuver, it'd keep her hands clean while getting what she wants out of it," he said, not sounding angry, just resigned.

"I'm sorry," Indy said, leaning her forehead on his chest. His chin came down to rest on her head before pressing a kiss to her hair.

"It was a risk I knew I was taking, Indiana."

"Should I call my dad right now and rat out her cheating, backstabbing ass? Although that'll probably make things even weirder with Dom and that's the last thing I need right now. Still, she's such a bitch."

"What did she say that wasn't true? We're together. You're seventeen and I'm not. Nothing to be done about it."

When Indy turned her phone on again, it lit up like a stoner and she tossed it onto the bed, laying back and staring at the ceiling. Finally, the messages stopped, but then it rang and a picture of Caroline's face with a photoshopped mustache and fierce eyebrows popped up on her screen.

"I am about to arrive. Meet me at the door," Caroline said and then hung up.

Indy thought about leaving her out there to rot on the doorstep, but the idea that Jack might see her first had her heading down the stairs and slipping out the front door. She didn't need Caroline in the house at all, not with all the tension swirling in the air.

She sat down on the steps, watching a few people leaving their homes for work, kids grabbing their parents' hands as they walked to a silver or black Mercedes sedan parked on the street, the day still barely beginning for most of London, but so much had happened for her. It felt like a week had passed since she woke up this morning.

A car similar to the ones she'd watched pull away stopped in front of the house and Indy stood up, sliding past the black wrought iron gate that enclosed the property.

"I suppose I'm not welcome inside," Caroline said as she got out of the car, her large tortoise shell Dolce and Gabana sunglasses almost completely taking over her face.

"I didn't ask," Indy said, leaning against the fence. "What's up?"

Caroline reached into her bag and pulled out a file folder. "I received an advance copy of the draw. It won't be announced until later today, but I thought you should see it."

"Who am I playing?"

Her mouth twitching a little in agitation, Caroline handed her a sheet of paper, a sketch of the tournament bracket done in Caroline's precise script. Indy scanned it, searching for her name and she found it at the bottom left side of the draw.

Indiana Gaffney (WC) vs. Penelope Harrison (4)

Indy felt her stomach knot, something she hadn't felt since Paris, except she wasn't about to go out on a court at a Grand Slam, at least not yet. Of course Penny was her first round opponent, because today the universe had it out for Indiana Gaffney. She huffed out a breath and nodded. "I'll be okay. Her ankle has been giving her issues since France. She's not even close to a hundred percent," she said, trying to sound confident.

Caroline raised her eyebrows so high that they actually appeared up from beneath her sunglasses. "If you think so."

"I do."

"Will you and she continue to train together?"

Indy shook her head. "Probably not."

"Good. We will need to find someone for you to hit with, preferably a man. I will speak to Dominic about it."

"Fine."

Caroline nodded, beginning to walk away, but after only a few steps, she paused and turned around and said, "Are you not going to ask me about the leak?"

Indy shook her head and shrugged. "I don't need to. I know it was you. You knew I wasn't going to run to my dad and you wanted to sign Natalie Grogan, so you did what you had to do to make that happen."

"I am sorry it had to be that way."

Pushing off the fence and letting herself back in the gate, Indy let out a small laugh. "No, Caroline. No you're not."

Chapter 14

June 22nd

The gathered crowd gave out a collective "ahhh" before applauding politely. English tennis fans were notorious for their sportsmanship, but even they were having a hard time staying engaged in the match and Jasmine didn't blame them one bit. The last round of qualifying for Wimbledon was usually an exciting one, a fitting prologue to the two weeks of world-class tennis about to be played.

She'd been pretty confident after the first two rounds as she and Natalie breezed by two decent enough doubles pairs, but they'd run into a brick wall when the qualifying final pitted them against Camille Mercier and Agathe Lambert, a veteran doubles team from France who'd been off the court for a while after Agathe had a baby. Now just Jasmine and Natalie Grogan were standing in their way to the main doubles draw, where some unlucky ranked team would have to face them in the first round. They'd fallen behind from the very beginning, dropping the first set 6-0 and now they were just one point away from losing the match.

"Match point," the chair umpire said.

"Cover the alley, I'm going out wide," Natalie said as they met at the center of the court, bumping fists before she headed to the baseline and Jasmine went into the service box.

Jasmine bent at the knees and at the waist, making sure to keep herself out of the trajectory of Natalie's serve and then upon the ball, making contact with the grass across the court. She bounced up to the balls of her feet, ready to react to the return, but none came.

"Out," the line judge called and Jasmine got set again. Natalie only had one second serve, soft and safe, basically a meatball on a platter to any halfway decent player. She watched as Camille stepped up into the court, deliberately shortening her reaction time. With a serve that soft, she could afford to move in and it would give her a huge advantage of any shot she got off, making it nearly impossible for Jasmine or Natalie to get to the return.

The soft thwack of the ball hitting Natalie's racket had Jasmine tensing briefly and then she sprung into action, watching as Camille wound up and fired a forehand directly at her. She pulled her elbows in and hit a short volley back to Agathe and a net battle began, short and quick strokes, wrists and hands flying fast, back and forth four, five, six, seven times and then a passing shot from Agathe, before Jasmine spun to her left, her back to her opponents, and blocked the final volley back, between where the two veterans had placed themselves on the court.

Both Camille and Agathe bounced their rackets against the heels of their hands in appreciation and the crowd, who'd been expecting the match to end, gave a roar of approval. Jasmine sucked some air into her lungs before turning and high-fiving Natalie.

"Wow," the younger girl said, "that was incredible."

"Thanks," Jasmine said, a huge smile on her face. It faded as she glanced up into the stands and saw Dom standing there, Paolo at his side, but no Teddy. She hadn't really expected him to show up and he hadn't been there for the start of the match, but she hoped he might just be running late.

"40-30," the chair umpire said. "Match point."

When Natalie missed her first serve again, Jasmine did her best, but the return on the second was too much, a cross court missile out of her reach for a winner.

"Game, set and match, Miss Mercier and Mrs. Lambert."

They all met at the net, shaking hands, including the chair umpire as well, before gathering their things and heading for the locker room. There would be no women's doubles for them at Wimbledon this year. Back down to the junior ranks, at least for now. She couldn't help but consider what would have happened if she and Indy had been playing together. They'd had a lot more training time together and Indy's serve would have been too much for both Mercier and Lambert. And it meant they wouldn't be avoiding each other like the plague.

They both showered and dressed quickly and silently. Losing sucked, but talking about losing sucked even more.

"I wanted to thank you," Natalie said, just as they were both ready to leave. "This was a lot of fun."

Jasmine nodded. "It was. I'm glad Penny suggested it."

"She did?" Natalie's eyes grew wide.

"Yeah, when Indy had to withdraw. Didn't she tell you?"

"I thought maybe you asked her to ask me and I thought how cool that would be to play with you and maybe qualify for the doubles. My dad didn't think it was a great idea at first, but I convinced him it would be. You're an awesome player and I knew I'd learn a lot. Maybe we could play together again some time?"

"I'd like that."

"Oh good. I was afraid you were pissed at me."

"Why would I be pissed at you?"

"After what went down a couple of days ago."

"Natalie, I have no idea what you're talking about."

"When I didn't sign with Jack Harrison. I mean I still wanted to sign with him, but my dad freaked like he was going to try and get with me or something. Caroline's good too, I guess. I know how close you all are and I thought maybe you wouldn't want to play with me after that."

"We're not nearly as close as everyone makes us out to be," she muttered and as the words tumbled out of her mouth she realized how true they were. She and Penny weren't friends, not really. They just happened to train under the same coach. Indy was…who knows what she was these days, things had been so insanely awkward, Jasmine didn't even know where to start with that. Jack had never been her friend; he was always away when they were growing up, and Teddy had checked out mentally since Amy Fitzpatrick had waltzed back into OBX. The truth was Jasmine was the odd man out and maybe always had been.

Jasmine pulled her racket bag over her shoulder. "Guess I'll see you around then."

"Yeah." She turned and started toward the locker room door, but she only got a couple of steps before she heard, "Wait, do you want to play doubles in the juniors?"

That stopped her in her tracks. She hadn't talked to Indy about junior's doubles, but maybe a little naively, she'd assumed that they would be playing together if Indy lost in the first week of the women's singles tournament. She turned around and faced Natalie. The girl was biting her lip and her eyes were big again, this time with hope.

"Yeah, that'd be great."

"Awesome," Natalie said, bouncing up to her toes, making her even taller than usual, towering over Jasmine. "We're totally going to win!"

"We'd have a good shot," Jasmine said. It was the truth. A little practice and they'd be just fine going up against even the best of what juniors doubles had to offer.

"I can't wait to tell my dad. He's gonna be so excited," Natalie said, pulling her phone out of her bag before nearly skipping toward the locker room door.

"Hey, wait. Do you have plans for tonight?"

"No."

"You're not going to the Player's Gala?"

Natalie shrugged. "I'm only a junior."

"So am I," Jasmine said, her brow furrowing. "I got an invite."

"You're John and Lisa Randazzo's daughter. Duh."

Rolling her eyes a little, Jasmine nodded. "Right, duh. Anyway, do you want to come? I have a plus one."

A huge smile spread across Natalie's face and she actually bounced a little on her toes. "Sounds like fun."

"Great. Give me your phone," she said, holding out her hand. Natalie handed it over and she typed in Alex's address. "Come by Alex's house at around seven and we can get ready together."

~

When Jasmine stepped through the front door of the townhouse, it was already a mad house. Jack and Paolo were watching a soccer match in the library, the volume up almost all the way but still not drowning out their commentary in both English and Italian. Dom, who'd left the courts right after her match saying that they'd debrief tomorrow, was chatting with Alex across the foyer in the kitchen. An older blonde woman Jasmine assumed was Alex's mother was sitting at the kitchen table listening intently. Teddy came flying down the stairs, holding at least five shirts, shouting for Jack's opinion.

He didn't even acknowledge her presence as she flew past her into the library.

"Hi Ted," she responded softly, knowing he wouldn't hear.

She took the stairs two at a time, though she wasn't quite sure why she was in such a rush. Indy, no doubt, would be in their room and things would be just as awkward as they'd been for the last few days.

Penny was just coming out of Alex's bedroom. Her hair was pulled up into a smooth chignon at the back of her neck, thin straps held the cream colored silk dress on her shoulders, a deep v-neck exposing a lot more than Jasmine was used to seeing from Penny. The dress was fitted at the waist and over the hips, flaring just slightly at the bottom. That famous necklace Alex had given her hung between her breasts. Girls like Penny Harrison shouldn't be allowed to exist in real life.

"Penny, I hope you and Alex don't mind, I invited Natalie over to get ready with us. She was kind of bummed about the loss, so I thought the party might cheer her up."

With a smile and a shrug, Penny said, "Why would we mind? Of course she's welcome. I'm sorry about the match. I heard you played amazing though. One of your net points made SportsCenter back home."

"Really?" Jasmine said, laughing. "That's pretty awesome. Thanks."

"No problem. I'll send Natalie up when she gets here."

The click clack of Penny's heels echoed down the stairs as Jasmine slipped into the room she shared with Indy and she sighed in relief. It was empty, Indy most likely still in the shower. She set her bag down and went straight to the closet where she'd hung her garment bag. She'd packed a few dresses, knowing she'd want options for nights like this.

The first was a short floaty strapless number, sweetheart neckline, cinched in just under her breasts with several layers of gauzy fabric that would fall unevenly around her knees. The dress behind it was a cream color similar to the one Penny had on, so she moved past it to the last one, a bright pink wrap dress with short cap sleeves and a black satin belt that would hold it together. Pink was her favorite color.

"That one, definitely."

Natalie stepped into the room, a bag in hand, tossing it onto Indy's bed.

"You think?" Jasmine asked, holding up the first dress. "Or this."

"The pink. You'll look super hot."

"Sounds like a plan," Jasmine said, taking it from the garment bag and laying it out on her bed, yanking her shirt over her head. "Can you get the door?"

Before Natalie could shut it, Teddy slid inside. "Whoa, sorry," he said, spinning around and facing the wall. "I just needed you to tie my tie for me in that awesome knot you know, the one with the layers."

"The Eldredge knot?" Natalie asked, as Jasmine slipped her dress on.

"You know it?" Teddy asked and Jasmine turned around just in time to see Teddy's eyes flicker down Natalie's long, lean frame, so much like Indy's except mocha where Indy was milk.

"My dad loves that stupid knot. He taught me when I was little. Come here," she said, crooking a finger in his direction. Teddy obeyed immediately, sliding the tie under his collar and stepping closer to her, not having to bend at all for Natalie to reach up and pop the collar of his white dress shirt with a thin blue pinstripe.

Jasmine looked away, tying the silk belt around her waist and adjusting it in the mirror above the dresser. She didn't need to watch Teddy turn on the charm with yet another unsuspecting female, but her eyes spied them in the mirror, Natalie's hands expertly weaving the silk of his tie into a layered knot below his Adam's apple.

She blinked and focused her eyes down at the dresser, grabbing her makeup bag and trying to concentrate on her eyeshadow options.

"Thanks," Teddy said, and she couldn't help it, her eyes were drawn back up just in time to see him squeeze Natalie's elbow lightly. "Save me a dance tonight, okay?"

"Okay," Natalie said and then Teddy was gone. "He's nice."

"Yeah, he's great." When he's actually talking to you and actually being a friend instead of only coming to you when he needs his stupid tie tied, she added silently, grabbing her foundation and forgetting about the eye makeup. Her hand wouldn't be steady enough yet anyway.

Just as she was about to swipe some concealer under her eyes, Indy moved into the room, wrapped in a cotton bathrobe, a towel still around her hair. "Hi," she said to Natalie, looking to Jasmine for an explanation.

"I'm Natalie."

"Yeah, I know. Um, I'm Indy."

Natalie nodded. "Yeah, I know."

"I'll uh, let me just grab my dress and I'll let you guys get ready," Indy said, shaking out a little pile of gold fabric she dug out from the corner of her suitcase and taking her makeup bag as well.

Natalie turned and grimaced. "Are you sure it's okay that I'm here?"

"It's more than okay," Jasmine said, shaking her head. "Come on, the cars'll be here soon. Let's just get ready. It's going to be a fun night."

~

The Wimbledon Pre-Party was mainly just a press event. There was a red carpet and a ton of photographers, but mostly it was just a chance for everyone to mill around and chat before the tournament got started in just a couple of days. The three cars that carried the coiffed inhabitants of Alex Russell's townhouse pulled up to the party just late enough to be fashionable and not obnoxious. Most of tennis's elite was already inside, but the photographers had stayed and as soon as Alex and Penny hit the carpet, it was obvious why. Tennis's golden couple was even more in demand in London than they'd been in Paris. They posed separately, but the crowd of photographers jeered until Alex stepped up to his girlfriend, wrapping an arm around her waist, pulling her close.

"Such a shame that's off the market," Natalie sighed next to her and Jasmine snorted.

"That level of hotness really should be illegal," she agreed with Natalie's assessment. "Come on, we're next."

"Allow me?" Teddy said, offering Natalie his arm, who took it without hesitation, her sky blue dress in an odd twist of fate, perfectly matching the pinstripe in Teddy's shirt.

Jasmine didn't even have a chance to feel that usual pang in her stomach as a warm hand slid from her shoulder to her elbow, tucking her arm into the crook of his. "You look beautiful," Paolo said and she felt the blood rush to her head, the sound of his voice making her shiver.

"Thank you," she said, following his lead as he started down the carpet, guiding her closer to the photographer's pool where Indy, blonde hair hanging in loose curls, that scrap of gold fabric actually a tube dress, was currently getting her picture taken while Jack stood off to the side.

"I wanted to ride in the car with you, but you were stolen away by your friend."

"She's excited to be here," Jasmine explained.

"She should be and so should you. Come on, time to get your picture taken."

"Only if you go with me," she said, smiling up at him from beneath her lashes.

"Naturalmente," Paolo said, leading her in front of the cameras.

The party was in full swing when they got inside, small groups standing at tables chatting, some people dancing, others sitting down munching on the free food.

"Come on," Natalie said, grabbing Jasmine's hand as the DJ cued up some house music, the bass pounding through her chest. "Are you two coming?" she called back to Paolo and Teddy who glanced at each other and then followed them out to the dance floor.

Jasmine let her new doubles partner twirl her in a circle before raising her hands over her head and letting her hips swirl in time to the music. It felt good to just let go for a moment, so she threw her head back and laughed. She'd worry about tennis tomorrow. Tonight was going to be fun.

The music was bad Euro techno trash, crap Jasmine wouldn't normally listen to, even if they paid her, but bouncing around the dance floor with Natalie, joined after a song by Paolo and Teddy, was a blast. She sometimes caught a glimpse of Penny and Alex, who'd squirreled themselves away in a corner being absolutely disgustingly perfect, as usual. Jack and Indy had pretty much embraced the idea that people knew about them and from what she could tell, they were working the room together, looking like two Abercrombie models who had escaped from the pages of the catalogue.

Eventually, the music shifted into something she recognized, a rap song from the 90s about clearing your throat that her mom liked to jam to while cooking.

"I love this song," Jasmine shouted to Natalie, but as the music shifted, so did the dancing and she felt two strong hands at her hips, fingers spreading across the material of her dress.

"Va bene?" Paolo growled into her ear and she nodded, stepping back into him a little, leading her body weight to settle against his chest, their lower bodies finding a slow, grinding rhythm.

Jasmine could remember being a little girl, maybe ten or eleven, and watching *Dirty Dancing* for the first time, wondering why anyone would dance like that with a boy, pressing sweaty bodies together to music that she didn't really understand. A few years later, she wondered whether she ever would dance with a boy like that. And now here she was, with Paolo's hand holding her loosely at the curve of her hipbone, the other trailing down her arm and as she pushed back against him harder, feeling just how much he wanted her. It wasn't scary or intimidating; it was sexy as hell and it made her feel powerful.

Just a few feet away, Teddy and Natalie were dancing as well, but it wasn't anything like what she was experiencing. She didn't want to see it anyway, so she turned and faced Paolo, meeting his blue eyes with her brown.

"Do you want to go?" he asked, his hands meeting at the small of her back. She knew what he meant. Did she want to leave with him? Go back to Alex's house? Find the closest flat surface and lose themselves in each other. Jasmine felt her throat tighten. She'd never done anything like that before, not really. The closest she'd come was with Teddy a few months ago and they'd definitely kept their clothes on. She opened her mouth, no idea what she was going to say, but then she felt someone tugging at her hand. Natalie was dragging her away from Paolo as the song ended.

"Come on, I need some air," the younger girl said, pulling impatiently until Jasmine followed. But she looked back quickly, an apology in her eyes as Paolo was swallowed up by the crowd.

They stepped out into a small courtyard. It was fenced in and mostly made of brick and wrought iron with a few tables scattered around, probably used for outdoor eating during the day. Jasmine breathed the fresh air deeply in through her nose and sat on one of the tables, letting her feet dangle. Natalie stood a few feet away, looking up at the London night.

"It was insane in there," Natalie said, moving closer.

"It was definitely hot," Jasmine agreed, though she really wasn't talking about the temperature.

"I'm sorry I let Teddy steal me away. He can really dance though!"

"It's fine, I..." Jasmine trailed off, about to say that she considered Teddy nothing more than a friend, totally fair game and that she was really happy dancing with Paolo. She preferred the simplicity of his interest to the set of baggage that came along with Teddy. But instead, Natalie cut off what would have been an impressive ramble with a short but shocking as all hell kiss to her lips. Her mouth had been open just slightly so she could speak, but apparently, Natalie took that as an invitation to slip her tongue along Jasmine's bottom lip and then briefly into her mouth before pulling away.

The shock passing quickly, Jasmine shook her head and jumped off the table, putting some suddenly much-needed space between them. "What the hell was that?"

"A kiss," Natalie said, "Are you okay?"

"Um, no, I don't—why did you—I don't like girls. One hundred percent straight girl over here."

Natalie wrinkled her nose. "Are you sure? I'm usually pretty good at picking up the vibes. You were so friendly and sweet and then you played it so cool and that was super sexy. Then you asked me to this party tonight as your plus one. I mean I just assumed, I guess, but this isn't a date?"

Jasmine tried to push her mind past the idea that Natalie thought she was gay and tried to piece together the clues from the other girl's perspective. It all clicked into place easily enough and she groaned. "I'm sorry, this is totally my fault. I didn't realize how it would look if you were looking for...well I mean...I didn't know that you were...and I can see how you'd think...I swear I would have been more clear if I'd known you were..."

"A lesbian," Natalie finished for her, cutting off her stuttering. "I don't really go shouting it from the rooftops, some people are still weird about it, but yeah, I am."

"I'm not."

Natalie laughed and nodded. "Yeah, that's pretty clear now."

"I mean, if I were, you'd probably be my type, but I'm not, and I don't want you to think..."

"Jasmine, It's fine. I mean, we're cool right? No weirdness?"

"No, we're fine. I mean, it was a little weird and I'm kind of flattered and oh God, Teddy's going to be so disappointed."

"I did notice that he was a little...interested?"

"Yeah, I think so...maybe."

Natalie sighed. "And to think, a few minutes ago I felt sorry for him thinking he'd realize you were into girls."

Jasmine didn't quite understand what she meant, but she shrugged. "Look, this doesn't mean that we can't enjoy the party, right? We can go dance some more."

"I'm putting up a good front right now, but I'm actually kind of mortified and I think I'm just going to head back to the hotel."

"Are you sure?"

"Positive. Have Dom call my dad okay? They can schedule some doubles training time before the tournament starts."

"Sounds good to me."

Natalie disappeared inside, but Jasmine stayed where she was. The day just kept getting more and more surreal. She just needed to be by herself for a few minutes before facing the pulsing beat of the music and the intensity of Paolo's attention. Maybe it had all been too much for one day. Maybe it was just time to call it a night.

She made her way back inside and almost immediately Paolo found her. "You disappeared," he said, frowning, not looking put out, but definitely confused.

"I think…I think I just want to get out of here, if that's okay?"

He nodded. "Of course, I'll get a car to take us."

Jasmine felt her heart skip a beat in panic. Did he think that she was trying to pick up right where they left off? That she was asking him to leave with her? "Oh, no, you don't have to leave if you don't want to."

He must have heard the anxiety in her voice, in the raise in pitch, in the speed of her words. "Jasmine, relax. I want to go as well. I've had enough of this party and we are going to the same place, no?" He nodded his head to a man standing at the door and guided her toward the exit with a hand at her back.

"Hey guys," Teddy said from just behind them, jogging to catch up. "Mind if I catch a ride back with you?"

Paolo looked to Jasmine, but she just shrugged and got in the taxi the valet had hailed for them. Paolo followed and then finally Teddy piled in behind them. Shifting beside her to make room, Paolo raised his arm and let it hang around her, his hand falling against shoulder.

The ride was silent, but clearly somewhere during the trip Teddy had come to the conclusion that they hadn't just been leaving at the same time, but that they'd been leaving together. His arms were crossed over his chest and every thirty seconds or so he'd try to look past Paolo and catch Jasmine's eye. She sat further back in the seat, avoiding his gaze, but bumping Paolo's chest accidentally. "Sorry," she whispered, not really feeling sorry for the unexpected contact.

"It is okay," he said, but his hand released her shoulder and grasped the seatback instead.

The driver came to a halt at Alex's house and Paolo reached forward to pay at the same time as Teddy.

"I've got it, man," Teddy said, "I butted in on the ride. Only fair I pay."

Paolo shrugged and pocketed the money as Teddy paid the driver. Jasmine got out on the street, ready to just call it a night, but Teddy intercepted her before she could reach the gate.

"Can we talk for a second?" he asked. Paolo raised an eyebrow at her and she nodded. With a shrug he retreated into the house and the car pulled away, leaving them alone on the street.

"You like that guy?" Teddy asked, stuffing his hands in his pockets and rocking back on his heels.

"Yeah, I think I do."

"I don't like him."

"I don't care if you don't like him, Ted. It's none of your business who I like."

"Yeah it is. I'm your friend."

"Are you? Because from where I'm standing, it doesn't really seem like it. You totally checked out on me as soon as Amy showed up and in case you missed it, I've been going through a ton of shit since then and you've been completely MIA for all of it."

"You seem like you're doing just fine."

"Yeah, well, I'm tougher than I look."

"I'm starting to see that."

"Good."

"So…"

"So, I'm going to bed."

"Whose bed?"

Jasmine swallowed back a shriek of frustration. She was going to her own bed to curl up and fall asleep, but that wasn't the point. "None of your business," she gritted out from between her teeth.

"Jas, guys like that…."

"Guys like what? Guys who are interested in me, Ted? Guys who don't just like me as a friend? Guys who might want me? I said it's none of your business. You're my friend. You're not my brother or my boyfriend, you don't get a say."

"What if I want a say?" he asked, stepping a little closer.

She stepped back, keeping the distance between them. "It's too late for that."

"Since when?"

"Since you decided it would be a good idea to sleep with Amy again. Since you asked Indy to keep it from me. Since you told me we were better off as friends. You can't have it both ways, Teddy. It's not fair."

"I didn't know she told you. You didn't say anything."

"What was I supposed to say? That you're an idiot for going back to her? You are, but it's not any of my business, right? I'm not your girlfriend.

I'm your *friend*. You've made that perfectly clear, so me and Paolo, whatever we are, that's none of your business either."

"Jas," he said, running a hand over the back of his neck and focusing his eyes down at the concrete sidewalk. "You're right."

"I am?"

"You are. You're right. I can't just…I'm sorry."

An apology. That was something, at least. "Okay," she said and moved toward the front gate. He didn't follow. "Are you coming inside?"

"No, I'm going to take a walk around the block. Clear my head."

"Oh, okay. Good night, Ted."

"Good night, Jas."

He spun on his heel and headed down the curving street, hands shoved in his pockets again and Jasmine couldn't help but feel like that good night had felt an awful lot like a goodbye.

Chapter 15

June 24th

"I have a match this afternoon. This is a really, really bad idea," Penny managed to say between gasps for breath as Alex dragged his tongue along the line of her neck, his hands gripping each thigh, holding them firmly around his waist. She'd fallen back against the pillows, completely spent just seconds before, her body singing notes that would make Mariah Carey jealous.

"Yeah, you said earlier," Alex murmured against her neck, his body shuddering against hers and then finally falling a little, catching himself on his elbows above her, their skin, slick with sweat sticking together.

She ran a fingertip down his back and he shifted to the side, falling back onto the mattress, dragging her with him as he went.

"Sorry Dom, I faded in the 3rd set because Alex couldn't keep his hands off me."

He snorted and kissed the top of her head. "Sorry Dom, Alex is a sexy beast. I couldn't help myself this morning. Either time." She laughed and pressed a kiss to the nearest skin she could find, his collarbone. "You feel better now?" he asked, wrapping his arm more tightly around her waist, adjusting his bicep under her head.

"There wasn't anything wrong."

"Try again, Penelope," he said, swatting her backside lightly.

"Mmm," she hummed, "okay, maybe I've never...I haven't...." She sighed, trying to put into words what she was feeling. "Even though we're fighting or whatever, Indy's my friend."

"She is," Alex agreed.

"I've never played a friend in a match this important before. In fact, I've never played a match against a friend, ever."

"You been holding this in since you found out?"

Penny shrugged. "Maybe." It wasn't that she was afraid of Indy on the court. Practice had been going well and her reactions were much better than the day they'd practiced together, but still, something was niggling away at her, something she'd never felt before going into a match.

"Does it help that you're hacked off at her?" Alex asked.

"I don't know, maybe? Is that bad?"

"You don't have a bad bone in your body, love. Not one."

"You're biased," she said. "Very biased."

"I thought it before any of this. Everyone knows it."

"Fine, we'll debate that another time. How do you do it then?"

"What? Play against your friends?"

"No. Win against your friends."

"Simple. You want to win. So does she. Go out and play your hardest. Don't disrespect her and your friendship by allowing it to get in the way of what you both want. You really never played against any of your friends when you were little?"

She shrugged. "I didn't really have a lot of time for friends until recently and now…"

"And now you have one and she lied to you." She nodded against his chest. "People let you down quite a lot, don't they?"

"I think I expect too much."

"You don't," he said, forcefully, his hand gripping her hip a little bit tighter. "You don't expect too much, not from your brother, not from Indy and certainly not from me. No argument, okay?"

She wanted to argue and she wanted to know why he felt this way about her, why he'd put her up on such a high pedestal, but his voice was so fierce and so fragile at the same time, she couldn't do anything except say, "Okay."

"Good, now come on," he said, "up you get. You've got a match this afternoon." He released her and she rolled away, scooting off the bed, not bothering to grab a sheet to cover up as she walked toward the en suite bathroom. She could feel his eyes following her as she walked away, so she stopped at the door and glanced back over her shoulder.

"Coming?" she asked and then kept walking, knowing in a moment she'd heard the creak of the bed springs as he got up to join her.

~

Penny sat on the trainer's table and checked her rackets, running her fingers slowly over the strings of each one before placing them in her bag, white with a gold, glittery Nike swoosh across the side. Her outfit matched, a white fitted tank and a traditional white pleated tennis skirt, both with the same gold, glittery Nike swoosh logo. Wimbledon's dress regulation of white only on the court fit well with her own personal preferences.

"Are you sure about this?" Dom asked from across the trainers' room.

"Your ankle really feels okay?" Jack asked anxiously.

She looked back and forth between both of them and then let her eyes slide over their heads to where Alex was leaning against the wall in the far corner, arms crossed over his chest, mouth firmly shut.

"Why don't you guys go check on Indy?" she suggested, deliberately not answering either of them. It had nothing to do with her ankle, they were just stressing out. "If I know her, she's freaking out right about now and could use a little of your support."

Dom rolled his eyes, but nodded and patted her on the shoulder as he walked by. Jack didn't move.

"You sure?" he mumbled. Now it had nothing to do with her ankle. She could see the battle raging across his face, a war between being there for his littler sister and checking on his girlfriend.

"Bro, go see her before she throws up on her new white dress."

Jack exhaled sharply through his nose and nodded. "See you after, Pen."

The door clicked shut behind him and Alex finally pushed off the wall, moving straight for her. "I won't ask how your ankle feels and I won't ask if you're sure you want to play. I know you and it's not in you to withdraw. So I'm just going to say good luck."

Penny reached out and took his hands in hers. "Thank you."

He lifted one hand to his lips and kissed the back of it, then stepped away, leaving the room without a backward glance. She knew he was heading for the stands on Court 1, the second largest court on the grounds. She'd only have a few more minutes to wait before they'd be ready to march out for the match.

Just to be sure, she rotated her ankle and didn't feel anything then she twisted it in the other direction and again, nothing. With no pain to worry about, at least not yet, she let her mind drift to her practice session with Indy just a few days ago, before she found out what her friend and her brother had been keeping from her. Indy's serve had been particularly good that day, but there'd been no pressure, no urgency for the inexperienced player. They'd just been out there having fun and getting their work in.

Today would be a different story entirely. She didn't expect Indy to revert completely back to the bundle of nerves she'd been on the court when she first arrived at OBX, but first round at Wimbledon would definitely unnerve her. Beyond that though, Penny knew she hadn't been at her sharpest that day. A few practice sessions with Alex between then and now had gotten her to where she wanted to be for the match. It was possible, just based on that last training session that Indy would be a little over-confident. The mental game was important, especially at this level when physical skills were so often equal.

A knock at the door drew her from her thoughts. "Miss Harrison," a court attendant called, "we're ready for you."

Slinging her racket bag over her shoulder and adjusting her ponytail, she slipped through the door, nodding to the attendant, a heavy-set, red-headed woman in an official Wimbledon blazer who smiled and said, "This way, please."

She followed her down the long corridor and then briefly out onto the grounds where a security official joined them for the walk to Court 1. The crowd meandering down the paths toward the courts parted for them, some fans wishing her luck as she went by. Penny caught a glimpse of Indy's long blonde ponytail up ahead of her as she followed her own security guard onto their court.

"Ladies and Gentlemen," an announcer called to the fans already at the court. "Miss Indiana Gaffney, a tournament wildcard and Miss Penelope Harrison, our number four seed, both ladies of the United States of America."

The crowd hadn't fully arrived yet and those who were there hadn't completely settled into their seats, but Penny ignored them. She might have some fans cheering for her because of her connection to Alex and what happened in France, but most tennis fans, especially in the early rounds of a tournament, wanted one thing, a long match and the underdog coming out on top. She couldn't rely on fan support. She needed to just go out and play her best. It was time to focus.

The ball boy brought her a few options and she nodded at Indy across the court as they both began to warm up their serves, falling easily into the pre-match routine they learned while training at OBX.

Her muscles loosened up easily and, as was normal during a match at a Grand Slam, time sped up. Before she knew it, the chair umpire called them to the center of the court. Penny grabbed a quick drink at her chair and then headed to the meeting at the net.

Indy was already there, bouncing on the balls of her feet, her extra energy radiating off of her in waves.

"Ladies," the umpire greeted them. "Miss Gaffney, please call it in the air." He flipped the large silver coin into the air.

"Heads," Indy called out.

Tails never fails, Penny thought to herself and grinned when the coin landed on tails.

"Miss Harrison?" the umpire asked, picking up the coin.

Penny flicked her eyes to Indy. "You can serve," she said, the first words she'd uttered to her friend since the other day. When she found out she'd be playing Indy, it had felt a little like the walls were closing in on them at Alex's. Running into each other in the hallways, in the kitchen, going to and from practice sessions and poor Jack caught in the middle, even though that was his own damn fault. He should have told her right away; they both should have.

Indy tilted her head, confusion slipping over her features, but then she smiled. "Let's go."

"Let's," Penny agreed and offered her hand. They shook and then they both shook the umpires hand before retreating to their respective baselines. As she did, examining her racket closely, Penny felt something loosen in her chest and shoulders, something she hadn't realized was knotted tightly until that moment. She kept her back to the court, pulling her necklace out from beneath her shirt, letting the dull bronze penny sit in the center of her palm. Squeezing it in a fist, she kissed the fingers wrapped tightly around it and then tucked it back inside.

She turned as Indy was tossing a ball back to the ball boy and the chair umpire looked up from his score sheet and said, "Play."

Keeping her toes at the baseline, Penny shifted her weight to the balls of her feet, rocking gently from side to side before bending over slightly at the waist. Most of Indy's opponents would give the hard serving player a feet few of space beyond the baseline. Those extra feet would give Indy's serve room to travel a little longer, slow down just a few fractions more before having to return it. Penny wasn't all that concerned with reaction time. She knew she could catch up to whatever Indy threw at her. She was more worried about getting her return back to Indy before she had time to react. Indy wasn't used to people being able to return her serve and her return game was a major weakness because of it.

The first serve was Indy's bread and butter, a screaming rocket down the center of the court, skimming neatly off where the lines met in a T, but Penny bounced out of her crouch in perfect position for a return and with a short, fluid forehand, an equally fierce groundstroke clipped the far baseline and sailed past a stunned Indy for a clean winner.

The crowd was silent for just a split second and then let out an almost collective sigh of appreciation and then applause. Penny could feel Indy's eyes on her from the other side of the court, but she didn't look up. This wasn't time to think about her friend or how they weren't friends anymore or anything else other than the perfect return she'd just hit and the statement it had made. For the best of three sets, Indy was her opponent and nothing else.

"Love–15," the chair umpire said.

Three more serves yielded similar results, though Indy managed to get her racket on the latest, starting a short rally that ended when Penny raced up to catch a poorly placed backhand in the air and slam it back for a winner.

"Game, Miss Harrison," the chair umpire said.

She had her break. Now all she had to do was keep it.

The ball boy sent her one ball and then another. Both were still looking good, so she pocketed one beneath her skirt. The other she bounced beneath her racket, getting a feel for it and keeping her feet moving underneath her, before stepping up to the baseline.

Indy lined up across the court, bent at the waist, twisting her racket between her hands. Penny took the ball in hand, rolling it over her palm before bouncing it once, twice, three and four times. Then bringing her hands together, coiling down toward the ground, she let her body gather power through her legs before exploding up and out, through the ball. A hard, flat serve directly into Indy's body, handcuffing her return, the ball hitting the racket frame and bouncing away weakly on the wrong side of the net. Just as the ball bounced for a second time, she felt a small twinge in her ankle. "Crap," she muttered under her breath but kept her face blank.

"15–Love," the chair umpire called and Penny grabbed the ball out from beneath her skirt as she and Indy changed sides, Penny beating her to the net and walking past her without looking up. She went straight for the baseline and waited for Indy to collect herself. She did so quickly enough, Dom's between-point routine training taking over, a few breaths, forget about the last point and move on to the one ahead.

Penny didn't want to forget the last point though, so ignoring the fleeting pain in her ankle and what it might mean, she piggybacked the previous serve almost identical to the last one, right into the body, as hard as she could. Indy tried to pull her hands in in time to return it, but again, it was a mishit, barely making it to the net before bouncing away harmlessly. The pain wasn't there this time, but still, she kept all emotion off her face. Indy wasn't a master of the mental game yet, but they knew each other pretty well, well enough for the other girl to read her face during the match.

"30–Love," the chair umpire said, and the crowd started to murmur uncomfortably. Six straight points for one player, especially to start a match, always created a certain uneasiness with fans. Would the match be a boring blow out, one player totally dominating the other?

"Come on, Pen," a voice shouted out through the murmuring of the crowd and the noise increased in apparent agreement. Maybe they'd be cheering for her after all.

It was time to switch it up a little bit, keep Indy on her toes. The next serve, off speed with some major spin on it, arched high through the air and kicked out wide, making Indy lunge desperately, but the ball was beyond her before she could get there. Again, no pain and she let herself, at least on the inside, breathe a sigh of relief.

"40–Love."

Penny finally looked across the net. Indy's face was crinkled, not in fear, but in confusion, like her body wasn't doing what she needed it to do

and she couldn't figure out why. She pursed her
lips. Maybe Indy was feeling the pressure, those
nerves that haunted her back at OBX and early in
Paris creeping up again. Whatever it was, Penny
was more than willing to take advantage of it. The
last serve she put straight down the center of the
court, going for the white T, the same way Indy
had with her service game. A little bit of anything
you can do, I can do better, played through her
head as the ball skidded off the white paint, past
Indy's racket, and then whizzed just by the ear of
the baseline judge.

"Game, Miss Harrison. Miss Harrison leads,
two games to love."

"Yeah," she let herself say, pumping her
fist, letting her fingernails dig into the palms of her
hand. The pain was back, this time a quick pulsing
ache that centered in her ankle and fanned out
through her foot and her calf. She moved to the
other side of the court, tossing a leftover ball back
to the ball boy as the crowd applauded politely. But
there was a buzz in the air now, not electric, but
radiating disinterest, conversations about other
matches coming up that day or plans for lunch
before the next match starting up between the
fans.

As she settled in to receive Indy's next serve
Penny pushed the pain down and refocused. There
was no way she was going to let a little bit of pain
make any difference in this match.

Chapter 16

June 24th

Indy shuffled her feet over the smooth, short grass court deep behind the baseline and blocked back Penny's forehand, a high arching lob toward the other side of the court. She twisted her body around just in time to watch Penny run forward and, with a swinging volley, bury a short winner cross-court. No chance for her to even move in the ball's direction before it bounced again.

"Game, Miss Harrison." Indy let her head fall back, the sweat beading on her forehead, spilling down her temples. The chair umpire had to be tired of saying that, like when you say a word over and over again, it starts to lose its meaning.

Miss Harrison was starting to become something else. She wasn't the girl on the opposite side of the court anymore, her friend, the sister of the guy she was falling for. "Miss Harrison" were two words standing in her way and just refused to budge. "Miss Harrison leads the second set, 5-0."

She knew Penny was tough, knew she was a great player. She'd seen it on her first day at OBX. Her serve had been taken apart thoroughly that day, but Indy figured she'd come a long way since then. She'd put in the time, the effort, she'd moved beyond raw talent to a more polished game, making shots instead of just hitting the ball. So why in the hell was the result the same?

She hadn't managed to hold serve even once during the first two sets, let alone even attempt to break Penny's serve. That was supposed to be her strength and it was failing her. There wasn't anything different about what she was doing. Her serves were hard and well placed, but she couldn't get them past Penny with any consistency. Her opponent would anticipate the location, the speed, everything. Was Penny just that much better than she was?

The question had plagued her for forty minutes or so and it was keeping her brain whirring; the only thing stronger than her nerves was the confusion. The only answer she'd managed to come up with was "yes." Penny Harrison was just that much better than she was, bum ankle and all. She'd underestimated her friend's abilities or maybe overestimated her own. Dom would know, but she couldn't ask him during the match as coaching wasn't allowed for players on the court. Even if she could, she wouldn't. Dom Kingston was pretty low on the list of people she trusted these days. But really, realistically speaking, it was just too late. Penny wasn't going to blow this lead, no matter how much her ankle hurt. Indy knew the other girl was trying to hide the pain in her ankle, but it was pretty obvious to everyone how much it hurt, grimaces flickering over the normally stoic poker face, if ever so briefly. That only made it worse. Penny Harrison, on one leg, was wiping the floor with a full-strength, top of her game, Indiana Gaffney.

The crowd had long since stopped paying attention. Mostly, it had thinned out, spectators wandering off in search of a more competitive match up and so the umpire didn't even have to ask for quiet as Penny stepped up to the baseline to serve out the match. A brief thought of withdrawing flickered through her head. Just walking up to the chair umpire and ending the suffering. It would help save Penny's ankle for the next round and it would just bring an end to this shit show of a match. It just wasn't the effort she'd want to give, even though she'd put everything into it. She'd dropped Jasmine for this. Her performance in the singles tournament was supposed to convince sponsors that she was who they wanted to sign for their tennis lines, to represent their brands to the public, and she'd gone out and embarrassed herself.

Indy faced the wall behind her baseline, straightening the strings on her racket. Briefly, she caught the eye of a line judge who kept her face blank, but Indy could see the emotion flicker in her eyes, pity, disgust, annoyance, boredom, or maybe nothing. Maybe she was just imagining it. She shook her head, trying to clear it of the insane amount of negativity that had seeped in while taking the beating of her life.

She turned away and stepped up to the baseline. Penny was ready and waiting across the court. Indy nodded that she was ready to go and Penny nodded back, then just like she had the entire match, she served perfectly, a laser beam into her hands. The placement was almost impossible for Indy to return effectively, her long arms a disadvantage as she had to draw them into her sides and try to get the racket face at a decent angle to hit the ball. She just barely managed it, but Penny anticipated a weak return and had moved up toward the net, easily dunking a soft volley across the court to win the point.

"15-Love."

Huffing out a breath of annoyance, Indy moved to the other side of the court, waiting for another serve. She just set herself into her crouch and waited for Penny to choose a ball. Penny didn't delay either and Indy appreciated her willingness to put an end to this misery.

Another serve, this one straight up the center of the court and Indy didn't even have time to flinch toward it before it nearly took the head off the line judge behind her. Penny's brow furrowed at her and Indy shrugged, moving again to the other side of the court.

"30–Love."

The next serve was exactly the same and Indy lunged for it, tossing her racket at it for good measure, but it didn't do any good. The fans who were left groaned a little and some people let out disappointed whistles. There was one sure fire way to piss off a tennis crowd and that was if they thought you weren't trying. Her eyes stung, tears gathering in the corners, but she pushed them down. Screw them. She was trying.

Indy felt the weight of Penny's eyes on her, but she didn't meet her gaze. She just waited for the final ax to fall. A spinner, up and away, completely beyond her reach.

"Out," the line judge called and Penny raised her racket into the air, challenging the call.

"Miss Harrison is challenging the call at the far service line. The ball was called out."

Indy had a good enough view of it as it spun by her. She was pretty sure it had clipped the line, so she made her way toward the net as the remaining fans clapped in rhythm, waiting for the replay to make the call. Penny was already standing at the center of the court, just beneath the umpire's chair, hands on the net, eyes trained up at the video screen.

The large replay screen at the end of the court showed a graphic version of the ball traveling over the net and just scraping the edge of the service line before bouncing away. It declared the shot, IN, in bright, white letters.

"Game, set, match, Miss Harrison, 6-0, 6-0."

Indy walked the final few feet to the net and held her hand out to Penny, who took it and squeezed it. She finally looked the other girl in the eye and nodded once before pulling away. She didn't want her pity. She just wanted to get the hell off this court. She touched the umpire's hand in what barely qualified as a handshake and moved over to her chair, shoving her racket into the bag and hauling it over her shoulder. She draped her towel over her shoulders and walked straight to where the security guard was waiting for her. Caroline was right beside him, her lips pressed firmly together in a tight line.

"Don't start," Indy muttered as the guard led them from the court grounds where, over the PA system, she could hear Penny giving a post-match interview.

"I did not say a thing," Caroline shot back. "You have a press conference. Be gracious. Talk about how well Penelope played."

"I think that's pretty obvious," Indy said as they approached the door to the media room. She set down her bag and nodded to the media relations official who introduced her to the crowd of reporters. It was mostly faces she didn't recognize, though she saw Harold Hodges, the man who'd interviewed her a few months ago mixed in with the sea of unfamiliar faces. He gave her a nod as she took her seat in front of the microphone, lights lining the sides of the raised dais, blinding her just a little, and waited.

"Indiana, your first match at Wimbledon, how did it feel?" the first reporter asked.

Indy picked a little at the white cloth covering the table in front of her. "Well, obviously I was excited and nervous. I wish it had gone better, but I can't wait to get out there again."

"Do you think nerves played a factor in how you played today?"

"No. I think Penny Harrison was the major factor behind how I played today. She was incredible."

"You and Penny are friends. What was it like playing against her in the biggest match of your career?"

"It sucked," she said, painting a fake smile across her face. "She's really good in case you guys didn't realize."

"How do you think you'll fare in the junior tournament?"

"The goal coming here was to win it and that's still the goal."

"What will you take with you from this match today down to the junior ranks?"

"That I'm really glad Penny doesn't play juniors anymore."

They all laughed and Indy nodded to the media coordinator who said, "Any other questions for Indiana?"

"Did the news breaking of your controversial relationship with Penny's older brother and agent, Jack Harrison, have anything to do with your performance today?"

Indy leaned forward in her chair and stared directly into the reporter's eyes. "Fuck you."

She stood up and grabbed her bag and made her way down from the dais and out to the hall where Penny was waiting with Jack and Dom.

"Good match," Indy mumbled, trying to slip by her, but Penny caught her arm.

"Wait."

Yanking free, Indy shook her head. "You beat me. Let's just leave it at that."

"Indy…" Penny trailed off and she felt her shoulders stiffen at the tone. She could hear pity in her voice. Penny felt bad for beating her, for winning, or maybe just for winning the way she had.

"Don't," Indy said, cutting her off. "Just don't."

She marched down the hallway, Jack, not far behind her. She could feel him following her, but she refused to turn around. She went straight for the locker room, but he caught up to her before she could go where he couldn't follow.

"Just go be happy for your sister," she bit out before trying to push past him.

"Indiana," he said again, his fingers circling her wrist and squeezing. "I am happy for Penny, but that doesn't mean I can't be there for you. What that douchebag asked was totally out of line."

Indy shook her head and tried to pull away, her pulse thrumming in her neck when his grip tightened. "Let go of me," she whispered.

Jack's hand fell away and he took a step back, staring at her, his eyes wide. He swallowed roughly and then looked away from her, his feet carrying him down the hallway away from her. Indy watched him go, stopping halfway down the empty corridor to punch his fist into the wall. At the sharp crack of bone against the wooden paneling, she turned and slipped into the locker room where she'd be just another wildcard who lost to a top seed in the first round and not the girl who'd managed to alienate pretty much every single person she cared about in the span of just a few days.

Her phone buzzed in the front pocket of her racket bag after her shower. A quick glance at it showed a few missed calls and accompanying voicemails from Caroline that she had no intention of listening to, and a missed call from Jack but no message. The grounds were still overflowing with people and she followed a security guard back toward the private entry and exit the players used. There were a few autograph hounds hanging around, but there was a car waiting for her as well.

"Miss Gaffney," the same man who'd chauffeured her to the grounds in the morning said, taking her bag from her. "Tough fight out there today, if you don't mind me saying so."

"Thanks," she said, sliding into the car and letting her head fall back against the cool leather of the seat. At least someone had noticed that she'd been trying as hard as she could.

~

The drive back to Alex's house, made a little longer than usual thanks to the midday London traffic, still went by quickly, but it had given Indy enough time to clear her head. She still wasn't over it, not really, but as the minutes ticked by and the post-match adrenaline had faded from her veins, regret had surged through her. It had been a long time since she'd lost a match and an even longer time since she had taken a beating quite like that. She'd taken it out on both Penny and Jack.

Ahmed, the driver, had kindly informed her that the Harrison's had gone home already and he'd dropped them off before coming back for her. She let herself into the house and looked across the foyer into the empty kitchen, and then into the library. There, she saw the back of a familiar head, dark, thick hair cropped close to his head, the back of his neck tan, as always, broad shoulders peaking up over the back of the dark brown leather couch, facing the far wall. The TV was on mute, but airing the current match at Centre Court.

"Hey," she said, as he lifted a glass of amber colored liquid to his lips, taking a long sip.

"Hey." He set the heavy tumbler down on the table in front of him and leaned forward, elbows on his knees as she came around the couch, sitting on the arm. She let her eyes drift to the TV but didn't really see the match.

"I'm sorry about earlier. I was being a brat."

He shrugged. "You lost. You should see…" he trailed off.

"When Penny loses?" she finished for him and he nodded. "It's okay, Jack. You can say her name. I lost the match and it sucks big hairy monkey balls, but I've got to move past it, right? I've got the junior tournament to focus on now."

"You do," he agreed.

"The house is quiet," she said, standing up, not hearing the pounding of feet or chatter that the crowded townhouse normally echoed with during the day.

"Everyone's out. Penny and Alex went to lunch just before you got back."

"You didn't want to join them?"

"I don't third wheel on my little sister's dates."

"So then, we have the house to ourselves?" she said, moving in front of him.

"Yeah." He looked up at her, his green eyes already dilated, the green bleeding into black. She lifted a hand and ran it over the top of his head and then moved forward, nudging his shoulder back against the couch with her hip. Bracing herself against his chest, she moved in, settling a thigh on either side of his, straddling his body. She just wanted to feel something good after a morning of bad. Hovering over him, she let her lips brush against his, tasting the bourbon he'd just sipped. Jack strained his neck, trying to prolong the contact, but she pulled away, a corner of her mouth lifting in a small smirk, which he wiped away by gripping her hips and flipping her neatly onto her back, his body holding her down against the cool leather of the couch. The seconds ticked by, breathing heavy between them, chests rising and falling faster and faster, but he didn't do anything, just stared down at her.

Indy lifted a hand to his cheek and stroked the line of his jaw with her thumb, biting her lip as he leaned into the touch, turning his lips into her hand, kissing the palm softly. Then she felt his entire body stiffen against her and his weight was gone as he sat back, taking her wrist in his hand, running his thumb over a reddish purple mark blooming on her fair skin.

"I did that?" he asked, his voice suddenly much lower, almost like he was struggling to get the words out.

"I bruise easily." It was the truth. She had new bruises daily just from a regular practice.

Jack pushed away from her fully, dropping her wrist and shaking his head. "I hurt you."

"You didn't hurt me, Jack."

"Indiana, you have a fucking bruise on your wrist from where I grabbed you. Shit like that can't happen," he said, pushing up off the couch and striding away from her.

"Yeah," she said, quietly as he left the room, his strong shoulders hunched over. "But I liked it."

Chapter 17

June 25th

Jasmine woke when it was still dark outside. A lump at the center of the bed, on the opposite side of the room, shifted. The mattress beneath the lump gave a short squeak, as Indy moved around and then settled again, blonde hair peeking out from beneath the covers. Jasmine carefully swung her legs over the side of her bed and tiptoed to the dresser she'd claimed, pulling out some training clothes. She changed quickly before grabbing her racket bag and silently leaving the room, closing the door behind her as gently as she could.

Movement at the other end of the hallway drew her attention and she nodded to Paolo, who was leaving his own room, yawning and running his fingers through his impressive bedhead. In just a pair of low slung boxer briefs, the tight V of muscles at his core pointing down past the elastic waistband and leaving very little to the imagination. His chest was lined with dark curly hair, blending well with his olive skin.

Jasmine actually felt her mouth water at the view he was presenting to her.

"You're up early," she said. "I don't think you've been out of that bed before noon the whole time I've been here."

"The only practice session I could schedule today was very, very early," he said. "Too early." His eyes were still unfocused and he was using the doorframe for support.

"What time?"

"Half seven."

Jasmine grimaced. "Um…that's right now."

"Merda," he grumbled. Her mind flickered back to the other night when she'd been giving off signals to Natalie that she hadn't meant at all and inspiration struck like lightning.

"You could come train with me," she offered before she could stop the words from tumbling out of her mouth. The way they'd left things a few days before was awkward, to say the least. He'd left her alone with Teddy and by the time she'd entered the house, he'd been upstairs behind a very firmly shut bedroom door. Left with two options, retreat to her own room or work up the courage to just charge into his bedroom, Jasmine chose the first. Then the tournament got in the way, their schedules on opposite ends of the clock, she'd barely caught a glimpse of him in three days. Except she wanted him to know she really liked him and what Natalie had said. That she'd given her vibes, that she'd been chill and friendly and sweet and it made her feel like she was interested. But that was nearly impossible to duplicate now. She wasn't interested in Natalie, that's why she'd been so cool and apparently sexy. Now she was just a jumble of nerves. "If you don't want to, I'd understand, but I have a practice session in an hour and if you need…"

"Sounds good," he said, falling back away from the door and closing it behind him, presumably to get dressed.

"So glad I could help," she said to the large oak barrier and headed to the bathroom to brush her teeth.

She was sitting on the steps of the townhouse, waiting for the car to pull around when he came out the door, setting his racket bag down and taking a seat beside her.

"Sorry," he said, bumping her shoulder with his. "I am a grouch in the mornings before I've had coffee."

"Its fine," she said, taking a deep breath and steeling her shoulders. "I'm sorry too."

"Perché?"

"For the other night, for not…I wanted to, but I…" she trailed off, shifting toward him, ducking her head to try and meet his eye, but he was staring out onto the street.

"There is nothing for you to explain." He said it so simply. No drama, no fuss. Except that she did need to explain herself, desperately. She wanted him to understand what was going on in her head. The only problem was, she didn't really understand it herself.

"It's not that I didn't want to," she began anyway. "It's that I've never…it's not…I don't even know what I'm saying."

Paolo finally turned and looked at her, their knees bumping, the rough hairs on his calf tickling against the smooth skin of hers. He took her hand. "I mean what I say. You have nothing to explain. We can go as fast or as slow as you like or not at all," he said, dropping her hand, letting it land on his knee, but his knuckles brushing against hers. "It is perhaps a little cliché, but the ball is in your court."

"I think," she said, putting her own hand over his. "I think slow."

"Slow it is then," he said, lifting their joined hands to his lips, but Jasmine pulled away. Instead, she ran her fingers over his mouth, trailing over to the side of his face before leaning in slowly and brushing her lips against his. His hand mimicked hers, cupping her cheek and with a soft pressure against her jaw, drew her closer, deepening the kiss that she'd initiated. His tongue flickered out against her bottom lip and she opened her mouth in response. His mouth lined up against hers, soft, but hot and wet. A real kiss, a kiss that could lead to something more if they weren't sitting outside where anyone could see. Except that as his hand fell to her hip, squeezed lightly and then drew her closer, the brick of the steps scraping against the skin of her lower thighs a little, she didn't care who saw. She just wanted to feel him everywhere, all at once. Her hands slid up the back of his neck and into his hair, the soft, dark curls twining around her fingers and it gave her a little leverage as she pressed up onto her knees, the brick biting into the skin there, but she ignored it. His hands fell to her hips, tightening against the flesh there with each stroke of her tongue.

He pulled back to breathe, their chests heaving. "This is slow?" he asked.

Still trying to catch her breath, she balanced against his shoulders and nodded. "I did say that, didn't I?"

"Maybe not, my English isn't so good sometimes." Jasmine smiled and rested her forehead against his. "Ah, that smile. I will kiss you every day just like this to see you smile like that." The smile grew and it felt damn good. She hadn't smiled like that in a long time, maybe ever. Was this what it felt like when someone wanted you just for being you?

The whirr of a car engine had them both looking down the street at the approaching black town car that had driven them back and forth to Wimbledon for the last few days. Ahmed pulled to a stop in front of the house and popped out of the car. "Just the two of you this morning?" he asked, raising a dark eyebrow at them.

Jasmine felt her cheeks grow warm as she realized they were still basically wrapped around each other. "Just us," she said, pulling away and straightening her clothes.

~

The grounds at Wimbledon were mostly empty, but the streets outside weren't. A queue formed nearly every night for the grounds tickets sold every day at the gate. As the car drove past the masses and through the gates, Jasmine saw security attendants making their way down the line to wake up those who'd fallen asleep during their overnight wait.

Gathering their things, Jasmine and Paolo went straight to the practice court. Her phone buzzed in her pocket and she checked it quickly. There was a text from Dom.

Prepping Penny for match. Will be late. Can call Sam Grogan, have Natalie practice with you?

Jasmine's thumbs flew over her screen. *Got practice covered. Don't worry.* She looked up and Paolo was stretching out. The air around them was heavy and humid, the gray clouds light and high, making for an overcast morning. But in the distance, dark skies were approaching, a sure sign that rain was on its way. Wimbledon was steeped in tradition, so many famous players had graced its courts over the years, but the thing it was perhaps most famous for was the nearly constant rain delays that could send the tournament schedulers to an early grave. Later in the tournament, it wasn't so bad, but early on in the first week, with so many players still in the hunt, one morning of rain could turn the rest of the fortnight into a logistical nightmare.

"What do you need to get in?" she asked, sitting beside him in the center of the court, stretching out as well.

"Footwork," he said, twisting his body back and forth before kicking his legs out and bending over them, pulling his chest to his knees. "I want to get my feet under me before my match tonight."

"Backhands for me," she said.

"Why backhands? They give you trouble?"

"Always, for as long as I can remember."

Paolo nodded, "You hit it two handed, yes?"

"Yeah. I need the extra stability from my right hand, the extra strength too."

"Let me see," he said, pushing up to his feet and grabbing his racket and a couple of balls from his bag. "What do you usually do?"

"Just drills, moving across the court and then from the center, varying up how far I have to go."

He nodded, jogging across the court and grabbing a basket of balls, rolling it with him to the other side of the net. She started her drills, keeping her footwork solid and sending backhands over the net just as she always did. She stayed focused on ball after ball traveling over the net so when they suddenly stopped, she snapped her eyes to Paolo and waited for an explanation, but he was already headed toward her, shaking his head.

"Everything you do with that backhand is perfect," he said. "Assolutamenta perfetto."

"Okay, I feel like there's a "but" coming."

"Yes," he said, standing in front of her. "They are terrible and you will be eaten alive by your opponents."

"Thanks."

"Come here, we will fix it," he said, crooking a finger at her.

"Paolo, I've been working on this backhand my entire career. It is what it is."

"You have never tried it one handed?"

"I told you, I need…"

"No, what you need is to use these," he said, stepping up into her space, towering over her, his hands gripping her hips just like they'd done on the steps not so long ago. "Turn your body, using your right hand only and use your hips and legs to drive the ball. It is fisica, physics. More momento torcente, more power, more speed on the ball."

"Dom…" she said, stepping away.

"Isn't here," Paolo said. "Trust me, if this works, if the shot improves, he won't care that it was me who showed you."

He moved behind her, his hands finding her hips again and Jasmine almost laughed at the cliché of the moment. Here she was with a handsome Italian man and he was about to wrap his arms around her, let his hands cover hers on the racket. His foot kicked a little at her instep. "Wider," she shifted her feet, widening her stance, "and a little forward," he said, putting a little extra pressure on her right hip. She slid her foot forward. "Bene. Now, stay balanced and on time, your arms go with your hips; don't lose the power in them. Feel that?"

She did. She felt everything. Not just that there was more power in her lower body than she'd even thought, but his chest lined up with her back, his thighs pressed right against her backside. "Yes."

"Bene. Now, try it without me," he said, stepping away.

Her skin tingled at the loss of contact, but she reset her feet and swung her racket, letting all her power flow up from her legs. "Like that?"

"Exactly. Let's see how it goes."

The control was amazing. Before, when she'd hit a backhand, she had a decent idea of where it was going, but sometimes her weight would shift or her shoulder would fly out and the rally would devolve into her scrambling around the court when her opponent pounced on the short, misplayed shot. Now, as she slowly used one hand, powering through with her legs to direct the ball, it traveled exactly where she wanted it to go.

"Good," Paolo said. "Full speed now."

He backed up just a bit and sent blistering groundstrokes to her backhand side. The first two she was able to simply block back, but then her feet got loose under her and she felt her instincts take over. Shot after shot was flying low over the net settling deep in the court, hitting corners and skimming off the baseline.

"Do you see?" he said, when he ran out of balls to hit, hopping over the net.

"I can't believe this," she said, staring at her racket. It was so easy. Too easy.

"You can dominate with that shot and no one will know it is coming. What more proof do you need?"

"None." She stepped closer to him and grabbed the front of his shirt. "You are amazing," she whispered, wanting to thank him, but her next words were swallowed up by his lips as he wrapped his arms around her waist, pulling her close. Jasmine pushed up onto her toes and opened her mouth when his tongue ran along the seam of her lips. The seconds slipped away and they were both breathless as they pulled away. Paolo nudged his nose against hers.

"Again, not so much with the slow."

"Slow is overrated," she said, pulling him down for another kiss, just as the sky rumbled overhead and raindrops started to fall around them, light and slow at first, but then heavy. In just moments, a torrential downpour exploded from the clouds, soaking them almost instantly. They both ignored it, the droplets of rain rolling over their skin, slipping between their lips as their mouths came together slowly, tongues chasing each other back and forth. Finally, they both leaned away.

"It's raining," Paolo said, wiping rivulets away from her face.

"It is," she agreed, slipping her hand into his. They gathered their things and walked off the court, still unconcerned about the buckets pouring down on them. The damage had been done, they were both totally saturated.

They slipped inside the player's lounge, drawing almost every eye in the place, crowded with athletes and coaches whose practice sessions had been cut short by the downpour.

"No," Paolo said, squeezing her hand in his. "This is no good."

"What?" she said, using her free hand to push her rain soaked bangs, which had escaped her clip, out of her face. She caught a glimpse of Dom in the corner and took a step back into Paolo, hiding herself. She didn't feel like talking to Dom, not even after the discovery they'd just made out on the court. He'd shoot it down and she'd be right back where she started this morning.

"Come on, we're getting out of here," Paolo said, drawing her eyes away from her coach and back up to him. "No tennis today, the forecast is nothing but rain."

"So what are we going to do?"

His eyes lit up. "Have you ever been to Italy?"

~

"You know, for a minute back there, I thought you really wanted to hop on a plane," Jasmine said, leaning back in the small metal chair inside the gelateria, the tiny Italian hole in the wall in London that claimed to have the best gelato north of the Alps. She let her tongue run over the spoon, making sure to lick every last bit of frozen strawberry awesomeness before digging in for another spoonful.

"Would you have come with me?" he asked, though his eyes were focused on her mouth pretty intently.

She smirked. "The way this year has been going, I really might have."

"I do not understand. You are at Wimbledon. You are one of the best junior players in the world. You are gorgeous and very, very sweet and you are so dissatisfied, gattina. It makes no sense."

Jasmine quirked an eyebrow at him and that little nickname he'd bestowed upon her. She liked the way he said it, his tongue catching on the g. "In your experience, do women make sense?"

"Touché," he said. "There must be a way to change it. Like your backhand. Tell me, perhaps I can help."

Jasmine regarded him closely, digging the little spoon into her gelato. She wanted to tell him, she really did, but that would mean admitting it to herself. Admitting that it stung that her parents didn't show the slightest inclination to be at Wimbledon during qualifying, that Dom's acceptance of her considering college, while he meant well, had felt like a betrayal, that Indy's decision to play singles was the right thing to do but made her feel like she was being left behind and that Teddy's total inability to be a decent friend had just made it all worse.

"You do not have to if you…"

"No one believes in me. No one thinks I can do this, except me and you."

"Fuck them."

"Paolo."

"No. Fuck them. My whole life they said I was too slow. My feet were slow on the grass and on the hard court, even worse on the clay. Too slow. Tardo."

"You're not too slow."

"Yes I am, but the trainers did not understand how to work around it. Did not understand that slow does not mean impossible. What do they call you?"

"Weak," she said. No one had actually said that to her, not out loud, but they talked around the point. They called her game not quite there yet or said that maybe in a few years, but it all boiled down to weak.

He hummed. "Physically," he said, letting his eyes travel over her, lingering on her naturally thin arms and skinny legs, "perhaps, but not mentally. You are strong where it counts and you play like you were born to it, which, gattina, you were."

"Just because my parents…" she started, but he cut her off.

"No, that is not what I mean," he said, leaning forward in his chair and reaching out to point a finger at her breastbone. "You were born to it here," his finger lifted up toward her temple, "and here. You have the ability. I saw that today, so what is stopping you?"

"I don't know," she said, trying to figure it out. It wasn't Dom or Indy and it wasn't her parents. They always supported her, had since she was a little girl, but they didn't believe, not like she needed them to. If they did, they wouldn't have been pushing college tennis so hard; they would have understood what she wanted for herself. But did she really need them to? She'd never thought about it that way before. "Nothing, I guess."

"Okay," Paolo said, sitting back. "So the goal is to play on tour, yes? Live in hotels and airports and play until your body gives out?"

Jasmine smirked. To most people, it sounded awful, but to her, that sounded like heaven. "That's the goal."

"Then you are going to need money. It is an expensive life."

She wiped her sweaty palms off on the soft denim of her shorts. "And how do I do that?"

"Sponsors," he said. "And to get those, you need an agent."

An agent. Going pro. Giving up her eligibility to play NCAA and just going for it on tour. It would destroy one option entirely, but that option, the one people kept insisting she hold on to just in case, it wasn't what she wanted. "An agent. Just so happens, I know one of those."

Chapter 18

June 26th

"Let's just finish up with some serves and volleys, okay?" Dom called out from the side of the court and Penny nodded, swiping her wristband over her forehead. She'd worked up a decent sweat during the practice session with Alex and she felt good about her match that night. Glancing up at the sky though, she doubted very much if her match would actually be played.

Grabbing a ball from the basket set up next to the court, she took deep breaths, the same way she would out on the court during her next match. Breathing deeply and slowly would help lower her heart rate if she was worked up after a point or by whatever situation she found herself in. Even though her blood wasn't pounding through her veins now, it never hurt to just practice the routine. The things she did during practice became second nature during the real matches.

Bouncing on the balls of her feet for a moment, she looked up across the court and let her vision blur out Alex's familiar shape. Instead, he took the form of her next-round opponent, Danjela Dujmov from Serbia. Bringing her hands together, she held the racket against the ball as her knees bent, all her power pushing down toward the ground and then erupting up and through the ball as her racket head made solid contact. She sent a low-lying screamer down the middle of the court, skimming perfectly off the edge of the T.

Penny raced forward, anticipating Alex's backhand block back over the net and caught the return midair, burying it as far away from him as possible. But as she took that last step and the ball flew exactly where she wanted it to go, her ankle spasmed and sent a laser-like flash of pain through the joint before it locked in place, sending her sprawling to the ground. A noise flew out of her mouth, half shock, half agony, as her ass hit the ground hard, knocking the wind from her lungs.

"Shit," she cursed, wincing against the pain. It wasn't nearly as bad as Paris, but it still hurt like a bitch. She didn't look up, but she knew Dom and Alex were racing in her direction. Two shadows quickly passed over her as they both knelt at her side.

"What kind of pain is it?" Dom asked.

"Can you move it?" Alex asked right over him.

"Don't try to move it," Dom commanded, taking her leg in his hand gently and extending it out toward him. Alex reached for her hand and squeezed it lightly, their fingers entwining against the smooth grass court. "What do you feel?"

"It's…it hurts," she admitted, not able to just shake off the throbbing this time. She'd done something to it.

"Come on," Dom said, grabbing her other hand. "Let's get you up and get a trainer out here."

The tour trainer was a slight man, maybe fifty, with white hair and a dark tan from day after day out on the courts tending to the athletes. Penny had seen him around the courts before, but she'd never worked with him. She knew that look though, the crease between the eyes, the twist of the mouth and the tsking of a tongue against teeth. This guy wasn't pleased with what he saw.

"I don't like that the pain increases as your sessions wear on. I don't like that you didn't consult anyone before starting up your training again. I don't like that you weren't being monitored when you started training again." The trainer sent a glare to Dom, whose eyes were narrowed and shoulders slumped, already blaming himself much more than the doctor ever would. "I don't like any of this. Playing on a tear like you are, you're likely making it far worse than it has to be. Just two weeks of full rest and you'll be healed. You should withdraw now. Fight another day."

Penny blew out a breath and shook her head. "And Zina Lutrova will be Wimbledon champion. Again. That's not going to happen. I'm not waiting another year."

"Penny, listen to the trainer."

She pulled her foot out of the trainer's grasp and glared up at her coach. "No, Dom you listen to me. I'm fine. I'm playing."

"Penelope."

"I'm serious, Dom. I'm playing, so either get on board with that or get the fuck out of my way." Her coach stood there, mouth open and eyes wide. She'd never seen him struck speechless before and the harshness of her words started to echo back into her mind. Maybe that had been too much. He meant well, he always did. He wanted what was best for her, but she wanted that too and if he couldn't see it, then she'd have to make him.

"Penny," Alex said, while Dom threw his hands up in the air, stepping away. "Come on love, this is…"

"It's an injury I can play through. A cortisone shot today and I'll be good as new."

"They don't always work," Dom shot back over his shoulder.

"If it doesn't, she won't play," Alex said before she could open her mouth to respond again. "Right?"

"Right," she agreed between clenched teeth. It was going to work. Simple as that. It had to.

~

The back garden in Alex's house was a small rectangle of slightly patchy grass with a black wrought iron fence separating his property from the homes behind and to the side. It provided a modicum of privacy in the middle of an ancient city. Green ivy, not unlike the stuff that lined the fences at Wimbledon, curved around the iron barriers. The sounds of cars, mostly a few streets away, but some on the road just in front of the house ebbed and flowed through her ears. It was almost like the beach back at OBX, where Alex had asked her to lay down and imagine herself winning at Roland Garros and now it was the only thing that could extinguish the fire running from her pulsing temples through her entire body.

She heard the click of the French doors behind her opening and then closing and bare feet thumping softly on the little stone patio just outside the house.

"It's not a court and we don't have the ocean, but I suppose this'll have to do."

"You can hear the traffic. It's soothing."

"Whatever you say, love. How does your ankle feel?"

"Numb. Won't really know until tomorrow."

"Did you talk to Dom? About what you said to him?"

"I didn't really mean it."

"Obviously. Dom puts up a good front and he knows you're pissed off, but it was probably a kick in the gut to hear those words from you."

"I'll apologize."

"Good."

"It's not as bad as that trainer says it is."

"You're a doctor now?"

"I know my body. I know how much is too much for it and it's fine."

"It's not fine, Pen, but if you want to play, no one is going to stop you."

"That's correct."

He rolled toward her and propped himself up on his elbow. Leaning over her, he let his fingers trail over her neck, hooking one around the chain of her necklace and pulling the coin out from beneath the collar of her shirt. He took it in his hand and squeezed a fist around it. "Just think really hard about what you want here, love. You've got the next ten years, maybe more to win Wimbledon, twice, three times, maybe four or five."

She brought her hand up and wrapped it around his. "Not six?"

"If you want to. If you make good decisions and take care of yourself and…"

"And don't play on an injured ankle because I'm too proud to withdraw?"

"I didn't say that."

"You didn't have to. If you felt like you could've managed the pain in your knee in Australia, would you have played?"

"Yes."

"See?"

"But that was before."

"Before what?"

"Before I figured out what was really important."

She groaned, pulling away, the necklace falling from his grasp, and rolled over onto her stomach, letting her hair fall into her face. "Don't get mushy on me now, Alex."

"I'm just saying that I was a mess back then. If my knee was hurting now and my coach and my doctor were both telling me that it was a bad idea to play on it? I'm saying I'd probably listen."

"I want to win Wimbledon. I'm in Lutrova's head. I can beat her."

"You already proved that to everyone."

"It's not about everyone. It's about me. I'm not bullshitting when I say that my ankle is fine. It hurts, but I can manage it and it's not a reason to withdraw."

"And if your ankle gives out on you?"

"And if your knee gives out on you?"

"Knee's fine. Doctor said so. Doctor's saying something different this time and he's a good one, wouldn't bullshit you. He knows what he's asking when he tells you to withdraw."

"You think I should withdraw too then. Just say it."

"Yes, I do. I think you want to win Wimbledon so badly that you're letting it cloud your judgment. I think you're making a mistake. A big one."

"You're just one more person I'll have to prove wrong then."

"I guess so." He sat up, squinting at the sky. "It's going to rain. Come on inside."

"In a bit. I'm just going to think a little bit more."

"Penny…" he trailed off.

"In a bit. I promise."

He disappeared inside the house, standing at the sliding glass doors that led out to the garden for a moment before moving out of sight. Penny rolled back over, her hands going to the necklace that slipped out from underneath her shirt. She twisted the chain around her fingers and pulled the coin into her palm. Slowly, she rotated her ankle out—no pain—then back in, a short, sharp twinge. Not so bad. It was like she said, manageable.

~

She crept up the stairs, using the banister for support, hopping as gracefully as she could from step to step. The second floor was dark, no light shining out from under any of the guest room doors, but as she turned, the door to the bathroom opened and Indy stepped out into the hallway. Her blue eyes were wide as they met Penny's. She knew Indy wanted her forgiveness, but at the moment, she just didn't have it in her. Penny managed a grimace and Indy's shoulders sagged before she slipped into the guestroom she shared with Jasmine.

With a heavy sigh, Penny faced the other end of the hall, the master bedroom door was cracked open just a hair, just enough for the golden glow of light to spill out into the hallway. A shadow passed by, Alex moving around the room, getting ready for bed. She'd been harsh, more than she meant to be, but they'd sworn to always be honest with each other after that fiasco in Paris with Caroline and those pictures. Be careful what you wish for, Pen, she said to herself, shaking her head and letting her bad foot rest gently against the floor. The pressure wasn't too terrible, the effects of the cortisone shot beginning to take hold in the joint. Still, she did her best to keep her weight off of it as she hobbled down the hallway. He'd given her honesty and that's all she'd ever asked of him.

She slipped through the doorway and whispered, "Hey."

He stood at the opposite end of the room, shirt unbuttoned, taking his watch off his wrist. As he glanced up, she was able to catch his gaze in the mirror. "Hey," he repeated.

"Listen, I'm sorry about…"

"Don't apologize," he said, shaking his head and turning around, giving her an even better view of the firm chest underneath the sides of his shirt falling open over his torso. "One of the things I love about you is that fire, Penny. If you weren't a stubborn mule, I'd never have fallen for you in the first place."

Stepping into the room fully, she reached back and shut the door behind her. "Can we...can we just ignore everything when we're in here? No tennis. No ankle. No Indy giving me the "please forgive me" puppy eyes. No pressure for you to win again. No pressure for me to win for the first time. Pretend like none of it is happening and it's just me and you, nothing else?" she asked, her teeth catching on her bottom lip as he moved closer to her, crossing the room in just a few, long strides.

"In here, it can be however you want it. You and me, though, we don't have to pretend. All that other shit, it doesn't matter. It's always just you and me, forever. How's that sound?"

"Sounds go-," but her words were swallowed up by his mouth, hot and wet and possessive against hers, his body colliding against her, hands falling to her waist to lift her slightly as he pressed her against the door.

"How's that, love?" he said, as he pulled his lips from hers, letting them travel along the column of her neck, biting down gently at her pulse point.

"Perfect," she said, sliding her hands through his hair. His mouth carved a trail of heat across her chest, his nose nudging the V-neck of her shirt out of the way, allowing him to explore the tops of her breasts, the lace of her bra finally impeding his path. Letting out a frustrated noise, his body shifted against hers, one arm sliding beneath her knees and the other bracing across her back, as he lifted her up into his arms, swinging her away from the door and toward the large bed at the center of the room. For a moment, she tensed, thinking he was about to toss her onto it, but instead, he kneeled at the edge, setting her onto the mattress easily. Her hands went to his hair, lightly running her nails over his scalp. He looked up at her, his hands resting against her knees, his palms warm and steady, his thumbs tracing small circles on the skin of her inner thighs. "Come on," she said, tugging at his wrists. She wanted to feel him, every single inch of him.

"No," he said, pulling free and fiddling with the button on her jean shorts. "I think we're going to try something new tonight."

"New?" she asked, and he smirked, his blue eyes flashing.

"Just lay back, love," he said, pushing gently at her shoulder with one hand, the other working open the button.

"And think of England?" she asked, letting her back hit the mattress and feeling the light pressure of her waistband give way.

"Yeah," he agreed, the rasp of his beard on the inside of her thigh and the warmth of his breath making goosebumps spring to life on the skin behind her knee. "Something like that."

Chapter 19

June 27th

The court wasn't Court 1. It didn't have stands lining the sides or a crowd that paid for tickets for her particular match. There wasn't a PA announcer or video replay or a security guard walking her from the locker room to the court and back again. And the girl across from her, though athletic and a very good tennis player, definitely wasn't Penny Harrison. Indy couldn't help the sinking feeling like she'd come down in the world. Like she'd gotten a little taste of what this whole pro tennis thing really was, but she wasn't allowed to have it yet, not really. So instead, she was on this outer court and for now, that would have to be good enough. The girl on the other side of the net, Zhang Li, was an up-and-coming Chinese junior, but while her game was solid, there weren't any weapons that really made it a tough match for Indy, not after facing a player of Penny's caliber.

"Time," the chair umpire said and she rose from her seat on the sideline and headed back out to the baseline. It was Indy's serve and aside from one game where her location had let her down and she'd double faulted her way to a break, Zhang Li hadn't been able to put together any sort of defense against her major weapon.

"Here we go, Indiana," a voice bellowed from the crowd and she let her eyes flicker, just for a second, to Jack. This was why she felt like she did about him, that intense, burning, scale every obstacle in the way kind of feeling. Things were awkward as all hell between them. They'd started something the other night, something that he maybe didn't really like about him or her or them. But there he was, supporting her because the awkwardness would fade, they'd work through it and he wanted to be there for her, maybe as much as she wanted him there. They'd work it out, the stuff that freaked him out or maybe the stuff he thought should have freaked her out or whatever they were going through. That was the plan anyway. Tonight, after she wrapped up this match, she wanted him all to herself. She just had to get through Zhang Li.

The match had only taken about an hour. Indy won two sets to love, 6-2, 6-0. Emerging from the locker room, showered and dressed, she saw Dom waiting for her, a large smile on his face as he pushed off the ivy-covered wall.

"Beautiful job out there today," he said.

"Thanks." She didn't really want to talk to him. She'd done a damn good job of avoiding him since they arrived in London and anything he said now would just ruin the good mood her win had put her in.

"The WTA is fining you for your outburst at the press conference."

"I figured," she said. "It was stupid."

"It was, but you don't exactly have the market cornered on stupid lately. I'm sorry I let you down."

Indy's eyes flashed to his. Maybe she'd let him have his say. "Go on."

"I want you to know that what you saw, that's over and I know it probably doesn't mean much now, but I'm sorry."

"I didn't tell my dad," she said.

Dom rubbed a hand across his face and nodded. "Thank you for that. She really loves him, you know?"

"I don't really care," she said. "I was...you're my coach and you believe in me, maybe more than anyone else has since my mom died and I can't...I don't care what you do or who you do or whatever, Dom. I just need you to be my coach."

"I can do that and one better, I'll pay your fine myself. If I had been the coach I'm supposed to be, that never would have happened."

"Thanks."

"So we're good?"

"Yeah, I think so."

"Great, otherwise this would have been really awkward. We're all going out to celebrate, on me."

"Define all?"

~

Jack and Alex weren't having any trouble keeping the conversation going between them. English and American football, a little tennis, a little business, some movie about gangsters that they both loved, the words flowed between them like old friends. It made sense that they'd get along, even when one of the men was sharing a bed with the other's sister. It was a brother recognizing that his sister had made a decision and respecting that decision, making an effort and realizing that she'd made a decent enough choice. Dom joined in with them easily and the awkwardness on the other side of the table was overshadowed by their conversation. The silence between the two girls, who should have tons to talk about, even if it was just how one kicked the other's ass a few days before, spoke volumes. Indy could barely stand it. It was her fault, so it was her job to make it right.

Maybe that could be the first step in making things right with Jack.

"Come on," she said, tapping Penny on the shoulder and flicking her head toward the edge of the private room Alex managed to secure for them at what Indy assumed was a ridiculously expensive restaurant. There was a small alcove that led to the restrooms and it would be perfect for this conversation. Contained and away from prying male ears.

"You really want to do this now?" Penny said, her eyes darting toward the three men across the table, all of whom were still chatting away.

"Yeah. Come on."

Penny leaned against the wall, arms crossing over her chest in a move so reminiscent of her older brother when he was annoyed, Indy almost laughed, but she managed to choke it down.

She took a deep breath and leaned on the wall opposite Penny. "I'm sorry about blowing you off after the match. I was upset."

Penny shrugged. "It was fine. You lost and losing sucks. I get it."

"I'm still sorry and look what you said the other day, about not knowing if you could forgive me or not."

"That was a shitty thing to say." Penny uncrossed her arms, one hand going to the chain around her neck, twisting it around a finger.

"I deserved it. I just thought maybe you'd had some time since then to think about it or at least…I don't know, not hate me as much."

"To be honest, I really, really haven't, but I don't hate you." It wasn't a lie. If there was one thing she learned about Penny Harrison in the short time they'd known each other, she gave it to you straight or not at all. Indy didn't really blame her though, with all the crap going down with her ankle, a fight with her brother's girlfriend probably wouldn't be tops on her priority list either.

Indy decided it was probably best to just lay her cards on the table. "Jack's your brother. You're going to forgive him eventually. What about me? Do you think you can forgive me?"
She didn't give Penny a chance to respond. "I know I should have told you. I should have just come out and told you."

"Yeah, you should have. I meant the other stuff I said the other day. I would have been happy for you. Why didn't you just say something? Like, just drop a hint that you liked him, anything?"

"I don't know. Maybe I was scared."

"Of what?"

"That you'd think I was using you to get to your brother or that you wouldn't approve or I don't know. I didn't think about it that hard. It just never felt like the right time to tell you."

Penny sat in silence, the seconds ticking by before she looked Indy dead in the eye. She struggled not to look away against the steely green she saw there, so much like her older brother's eyes it was almost uncanny. Penny and Teddy were the twins, but Penny and Jack, they were cut from the same cloth. "I think that maybe we weren't friends."

"Oh." Well, that settled that. If Penny didn't want to be her friend, well it friggin' sucked, but she wasn't going to beg anyone for their friendship.

"No, that's not what I mean. When you showed up at OBX, I saw a lot of what I went through in what you were going through so I thought I'd be nice. Figured I'd try to make things easier on you and then we just sort of were around each other a lot."

"That's what friends do."

"It's supposed to be more than that though, isn't it? I didn't have a lot of friends growing up, not really. It was all tennis all the time." Indy raised her eyebrows and smirked. "Okay, so not much has changed. What I'm saying is, we weren't really friends, at least not the way I always imagined real friends were supposed to be."

"I'm confused."

"We're supposed to have each other's backs, be there for each other and we're not supposed to lie or keep really big, important secrets. And we were sort of a pale imitation of that. Like we were playing the part instead of actually, you know, being friends."

"It didn't feel like that for me."

Penny flinched. "I guess I'm not really sure how to be friends with someone and like, let them in — not for real."

"You were doing a pretty good imitation of it."

"Yeah?"

"So do you think you want to try that, you and me, friends for real this time?"

"Yeah, just, on one condition."

"Name it."

"You never, ever, ever talk to me about what you and Jack do."

"I —

"Nope. Not unless you want me to throw up all over you and then you'd have to explain to everyone why. I don't want details about that stuff. I mean it. Ever."

"I think I can do that."

"Just…"

"Yeah?"

"You guys, you're happy?"

"We are. I think…no, I know we are. Your brother, he's…I…I think…"

Penny laughed a little, but then reached out, grabbing her hand. "I'm about to be really cheesy," she warned and Indy quirked an eyebrow. "Maybe we weren't meant to be friends."

"No?"

"Maybe we were meant to be sisters."

"Oh God, Penny."

"I know, I know, but I thought it and I just had to say it."

"Lets get back before they think we killed each other or something."

~

They wandered home late that night, the streets almost empty as their car pulled in front of Alex's house. No one had a match the next day, so more than a little bit of alcohol had flowed at the table. Alex was draped over Penny's shoulders, mostly holding himself up, but definitely needing her to guide him up the stairs. She stole the house keys from him and Indy watched as he leaned on the door and nearly fell through when Penny pushed it open.

"I better get him upstairs," Penny said, letting him wind an arm around her shoulders again, taking most of his weight, which probably wasn't all that great for her ankle "Night guys."

"G'night" Alex called over his shoulder as they climbed the stairs.

She looked back over her shoulder at Jack, who was giving the driver instructions for the next morning, safely assuming that no one would be in the mood to head in for practice until the afternoon. Leaning on the doorframe, she waited for him to jog up the front steps and gave him a small smile as he joined her, pulling the door shut behind them.

"That was nice," she said, as he looked anywhere but into her eyes. "Jack."

"It was," he said and then let out a shaky breath.

"Are we really going to do this again? You pulling away just when things get interesting?"

"No, I…that's not. Damn it. How do you put up with me?"

Indy laughed. "Are you serious?"

"Every time we get somewhere, every damn time, I make you feel like shit about what we have and I swear, Indiana, that's not what I want to do."

"What do you want to do?"

He looked down at the shining wood floors of the foyer. "With you?" he asked, though clearly he didn't require a response. Looking up at her with an arched brow. "I want to do everything. I've wanted all of you from the first moment I saw you. I want to know every crazy ass thought that pops in your head. I want to be there for your first tour win. I want to be there the first time you lose in a final. And I want you there with me for everything, Indiana."

"Is that all you want?"

"You know what I want," he said, reaching out and taking her hand, lifting up the wrist that sported a bruise for a few days. He kissed the skin, now totally unblemished. "And I know what you want and God help me, I'm trying to be a damned gentleman about it, Indiana, but you make it so…"

"Hard?" she asked, totally unable to control the giggling that followed.

"Yeah," he agreed, a short laugh pushing out of his chest, but he stepped forward, leaning over her. "Everything about this has been damn hard, hasn't it?"

"Because you insist on making it that way. I swear, Jack, sometimes it feels like you…"

"What?"

"That you like the drama of it all. Am I dating a closet drama queen?"

She could see the laughter still in his eyes, but his voice was firm and serious. "That's not it."

"No?"

"No. You just drive me insane…"

"Jack?" she said, wrapping her fingers into the front of his shirt.

"Yeah?"

"No more talking."

"Right," he said, closing the last few inches between them and slanting his mouth over hers. The kiss was bruising, a clash of lips and tongues and teeth, none of the finesse she'd come to expect from him and as he pressed his body into hers, he pulled his mouth away to whisper against her lips. "I heard what you said when I walked out on you that day. You said that you liked it. Did you mean it, Indiana?" His fingers pushed at the small of her back, angling his body so that his thigh slipped between hers.

"Yes," she whispered, her breath coming shallow and fast.

"Good, that's all I want you thinking about tonight. How much you want this, how much I want you," he said, stepping away from her and smoothing down the front of his shirt.

"You're kidding me. Jack, you can't just…"

"There's no privacy. Teddy's in my room. Jasmine's in yours."

"Crap."

"Exactly."

"We could go to the Dorchester."

"Where there are no rooms and where the press is probably camped out at the bar by now just waiting for someone to come stumbling in?"

"After I win. We'll go some place, just the two of us and my next trophy."

Jack smiled, his green eyes lighting up. "I like the way you think."

Chapter 20

June 28th

Jasmine raised her hand to the closed bedroom door. It was very early, the time of day where the only people awake are the people coming off a night shift and those early travelers, headed to an airport or a train station before the massive crowds descended upon the city. She let her knuckles rap against the solid barrier lightly, hoping that would be enough to rouse the sleeping man on the other side. Soft footfalls padding on the other side of the door gave her hope and then it was dashed when a sleepy, harassed looking Teddy Harrison pulled open the door, squinting at her as he rubbed at his eyes. He wore only a pair of thin cotton boxers, his chest bare, a nod to the warm nights they'd been having and the expanse of tan skin lined with lithe muscle drew her eyes to where she didn't want them to go. Quickly, she locked her gaze onto his face before he noticed.

"Jas?" he rasped. "Everything okay?" His eyes narrowed as they focused on something behind her.

She turned back over her shoulder where Paolo was leaning against the opposite wall, legs crossed at the ankle, waiting.

"Everything's fine, Ted. Is Jack awake?"

"Jack?" Teddy blinked at her and then again looked at Paolo.

"Yes, your brother. We need to talk to him."

"Now? It's like five in the morning."

"Four thirty actually," she corrected. "Can you get him?"

He rubbed at his face again. "Yeah, hang on a sec." He flicked on the light next to Jack's bed and grabbed a pillow from the floor and flung it against the bare back of his older brother. "Yo, bro, wake up, you've got an early meeting or something." Teddy kept walking back to his bed and buried himself underneath a pile of covers just as Jack blinked awake. He squinted at them before fumbling with a pair of glasses on his nightstand and sliding them over his eyes. Jasmine had a brief pang of sympathy for Indy, ridiculously sexy and Clark Kent glasses on top of that. She'd never stood a fair shot at resisting him. He swung his legs out from under the covers and nodded toward the hallway. They stepped back and he pulled the door almost closed behind him.

"Morning," Jasmine said, smiling sheepishly and glancing back at Paolo, who took the cue.

"Get dressed and come with us, there's something we want to show you," Paolo said, putting a hand on Jasmine's shoulder and squeezing lightly.

"Now?" Jack asked.

"It has to be now," Jasmine said. "Are you coming or not?"

"Secret mission at the ass crack of dawn?" His green eyes gleamed from behind his glasses. "Of course I am. Give me five minutes."

~

The practice courts were empty. There were only a few security guards wandering around the grounds to keep out overzealous fans who thought sneaking in very early would somehow go unnoticed. Every shot echoed like a bomb going off as Paolo and Jasmine went through a hitting session featuring her brand new backhand. She hadn't shown it to anyone yet, hadn't even used it in her first matches in the junior tournament. She needed Jack to see it though because this was the first step, just like she and Paolo had talked about.

One more backhand, a pretty one-handed slice that spun off speed, but far out of Paolo's reach ended the session and Jasmine pumped her fist and couldn't help the broad smile on her face. The smile grew even larger when she turned to the edge of the court and saw Jack standing there with a grin that matched hers.

"Well that's new," he said, as both she and Paolo walked over to him, grabbing water bottles from their bags.

"Brand new," she agreed.

"I'm guessing you haven't shown this to Dom yet or he'd be here with us."

"Good guess," Paolo said, shooting a little water into his mouth. "Dom is a great coach, but he is blind when it comes to Jasmine."

"Familiarity can do that sometimes," Jack agreed. "So, I'm also guessing you didn't invite me here because you wanted my opinion on your new backhand. What can I do for you?"

"Sign me," Jasmine said. "I want to go pro and I want you to be my agent."

Jack fell silent, but he nodded. "Okay, listen. You turned eighteen a few months ago, right?"

"I did."

"You can sign a contract, but your parents will actually end my career if I let you sign anything without them present."

Jasmine pursed her lips and shrugged. "You represent Penny. There's nothing anyone can do about that and if you rep me, that's two athletes who won't ever leave you. My parents don't have that kind of power."

"Fine, I'm uncomfortable with the idea of doing this behind their backs."

Paolo cleared his throat a little, drawing their attention. "You wouldn't want to sign with someone who was comfortable with the idea, gattina. This is why he is the right choice."

Jack nodded. "Thanks, man."

Jasmine huffed at being overruled, but kept pushing. "Okay fine, I'll make you a deal."

"A deal?"

"Yeah. I have a match today against Adelaide Brennan. I'm assuming you know who that is?"

"Australian and number one junior player in the world, took the top spot after Penny moved up to the tour."

"Exactly. If I win today, we Skype my parents tonight and tell them I'm signing with you."

"And if you lose?"

"That's not going to happen."

Jack stared at her, a hard look, like he was trying to see through her, trying to see if it was confidence or false bravado. "You really think you can beat Adelaide Brennan?"

"I know I can."

"Good. You've got a deal, Miss Randazzo," he said, holding out his hand and she took it, shaking it firmly, but her eyes looked up and to the side, meeting Paolo's.

~

Jack left them at the court, tapping away at his phone and mumbling about having to put together paperwork. As soon as he was out of earshot, Jasmine let out a high-pitched squeal and punched the air. "We did it."

"Almost," Paolo said, though his smile was spread wide across his face, making his eyes crinkle, premature lines from spending most of his youth out in the sun, revealing themselves at the corners. "You just have to win."

"I know I can win."

"I know you can too."

"Thank you," she said, moving close to him. "None of this would be happening without you."

"Yes it would," he disagreed, though he stepped closer as well. "You would have done this eventually, but maybe I gave you a little push."

"A big push and I needed it. So thank you." She didn't give him a chance to respond this time, pushing up on to the tips of her toes and pressing a soft kiss to his lips. It was meant to be short, just a thank you, but he caught her about the waist and held her there, tilting his head and creating the perfect angle to hold onto the moment a little longer. He took her lower lip between his and kissed her firmly.

He pulled away and leaned his forehead against hers. "Non mi aspettavo," he said, trailing off. "I didn't expect to feel this way for you."

"No? What did you expect?"

"A pretty girl to flirt with while Alex trails after Penny like a little puppy."

"He's whipped, isn't he?"

"Whipped?" He chuckled. "Yes, but I am beginning to understand the appeal."

"Really?" she said, letting her hands play with the dark curls at the back of his neck, the silky strands, still a little sweaty from their practice session, sliding through her fingers.

He didn't answer, simply let his mouth fall to hers again, picking up where they left off, the hot slide of two mouths coming together and slowly breaking apart, the kisses shallow, but intense.

"You two might want to not do this in public. Never know who might be watching."

Jasmine broke away and turned to the fence where Teddy was standing, elbows resting at the top of the chain link barrier. His face was blank and unreadable.

"What are you doing here?" she asked, feeling Paolo step away from her.

"Someone woke me up at a ridiculous hour, so I figured I'd come down and see what all the fuss was about. Looks like I'm right on time to catch the show."

"Teddy," she began, but Paolo cut her off.

"Do you have a problem with this?"

Teddy stood up straight and looked at the other man dead in the eye. "What if I do?"

"Then you must get over it," Paolo said. "I think she has made her preferences clear. She doesn't need jealous little boys following her around after they've been rejected."

Jasmine let the words sink in to her mind and watched as they hit Teddy. Is that what was happening? Teddy was jealous. The idea seemed ridiculous. Teddy didn't want her, at least not the way she wanted him and he'd made that perfectly clear, but apparently, he didn't want anyone else to have her either. Looking up at Paolo, she realized that it didn't matter. She'd moved on and he was going to have to get used to the idea.

The fence rattled and for a half a second she thought he'd leapt over it, just like he did every day back at OBX whenever there was one in his way. Instead, she looked up to see his back to them, walking away, again, just like he had the other night after dinner.

"I'm sorry I said that to him. I know he's your friend, but I…"

"No," she interrupted. "No, you were right and it's good that you said it to him. If he's going to be this way, maybe he's not really my friend after all."

~

There were more people than usual for a junior match. The sun had finally burned off the clouds that had hovered for most of the first week, but the weather wasn't really what drew the crowd. It was the match-up. The number one junior player in the world and one of the favorites to win the tournament against the daughter of tennis royalty. As far as Jasmine was concerned, this would be the last time people showed up to watch her because of her parents. After today, everyone would see what she was bringing to the table, that her game was world class and that she was ready for the big time.

Glancing up to the stands, she saw Dom chatting with Paolo, who didn't have a match of his own until later that night. Behind them, Jack and, to her surprise, Indy sat, but then again, that made sense. Indy was scheduled to play the winner of this match and she'd never seen Brennan play before. It was a scouting trip, nothing more than that, though odds are Indy was rooting for her to win. She probably thought it would be easier to face her than Adelaide Brennan in the next round. Jasmine had faced Brennan before though, two years ago at the OBX Classic and she knew her game pretty well. The only difference now was that she'd added some velocity to her serve that made it tough for most other junior players to return, a lot like the game Indy played, the same type of player she'd been training with for months now.

All she had to do was to stick with the general game plan, block back the serve and run down everything Brennan sent back across the court. The other girl was bigger and broader and thus slower. Jasmine smiled, thinking about how her new backhand would probably be too much for her to track down on a cross-court shot. It wasn't going to be easy, but she knew she could do it and she knew that later today, she'd snuff out one of her options and go after what she really wanted.

~

The computer bleeped and the screen filled up with her parents' smiling faces.

"Ah, mija," her mother said, "we are so proud of you! What a victory!"

"Great job out there today, kiddo," her dad echoed almost over her mom. "That backhand was fantastic! Why haven't you ever used it before? What a weapon!"

Her mom immediately raised her voice and kept talking. "Why are you not out celebrating? Are you okay? I thought I saw you favoring your right leg a little bit?"

"Mom, I'm fine," she said. "I wasn't limping and we're not going out until later because Paolo has a match in a couple of hours and we're going to stay and watch him."

"Paolo?" her dad asked, his dark brows furrowing at the mention of a male name. Typical.

"Paolo Macchia. He's staying with Alex too."

"That's nice, Jasmine. You said this was urgent though, mija. What did you want to speak about?" her mom asked, her concern easily read in her tone, even if her face was calm.

"You guys know Jack," she said, grabbing him by his wrist from where he was hovering off to the side and dragging him into view of the webcam. "Now before you say anything, no it's not what you're thinking. He and Indy are still you know, he and Indy."

Her dad blew out a breath of relief, but she knew her next words would probably fire him up again.

Jasmine sat up straight, lifting her chin, and felt the confidence flow through her, the same confidence that spurred her on to the 6-2, 6-1 victory over the number one ranked junior player in the world just about an hour earlier. "This morning, I asked Jack to be my agent and he agreed. He's putting together the paperwork now and we're going to sign everything tonight. I just wanted to let you guys know before we put out the press release tomorrow morning. I wanted you to hear it from me."

Silence. Two people who really never ran out of things to say were completely silent and as the seconds ticked by, Jasmine started to squirm in her seat.

"Harrison," her dad finally said. "You approached my daughter about this?"

"No, sir," Jack said. "She approached me."

Jasmine nodded. "And Jack wanted to make sure we talked it all out with you guys before we signed."

"Fine. Will you excuse us for a moment? We need to talk to Jasmine alone."

Jack nodded and patted her softly on the shoulder before he left the room.

As the door clicked shut behind him, her mother shook her head. "I thought we spoke about this, mija, about keeping your options open, about being ready."

"I don't want options," Jasmine said. "I know what I want. This is what I want. It's what I've always wanted. Everyone else, they want options because they think — you think — that I can't do this. But I went out there today and I proved that I could. I'm going to be a professional tennis player and maybe I won't be number one in the world and maybe I won't win Grand Slams, but I'm going to try and if it doesn't work out, you guys can say you told me so."

"Jasmine, it's not about being right or wrong or telling you we told you so. It's about what's best for you."

"And I know what's best for me. I won't be happy at college playing girls like Amy Fitzpatrick and dreaming about being on tour while Indy and Penny are living my dream. I want this and I want to sign with Jack. He's done great things for Penny and I think he can do the same things for me."

"Jasmine…" her dad began.

"John, she says she's thought about this. Have you? Have you really?"

"It's the only thing I think about and I know I can do it."

Her mom nodded. "Then go for it, mija. We will not stand in the way of your dreams."

Chapter 21

June 28th

Penny's eyes flew open and she had to bite her lip to keep from screaming. Alex, in his sleep, had kicked out his foot and hit her ankle, sending an explosion of pain through her entire leg. She squeezed her eyes shut and clenched her teeth, trying to fight back the pain, inhaling and exhaling quickly through her nose. On the other side of the bed, she heard the buzz of his phone, an alarm they'd set the night before sending it vibrating across his nightstand.

"Pen, you awake?" he rumbled from the other side of the bed.

"Yeah," she managed to squeak out. "You grab the shower first. I'm going to get a few more minutes."

As soon as the bathroom door closed behind him, she slid her legs from under the covers and sat up. She stared at her ankle in the dim lighting fighting its way into the room through the closed blinds. It was swollen, like it had been recently, but not too bad. Still, it ached. Gingerly, she put her feet on the ground and again, the pain, agonizing and overwhelming shot through her leg, spreading quickly through her whole body.

"Fuck," she muttered. She didn't know how long she sat there trying to will the pain away, but Alex eventually came out of the shower and dressed. "Meet you downstairs in a bit."

"Yeah, you want a banana for the car?"

"Yes, thanks."

He was gone and she had to get up and get moving. She had a match today.

~

Less than a week. That's how long the relief from the cortisone shot lasted, through a second and third round match that she probably would have won even if she only had one foot to play on. Now the pain was back, even worse than it was on that court in Paris and as the trainer wrapped the swollen joint and eyed her warily, she just gritted her teeth and kept silent until he left the room.

The pain hadn't lessened as the morning wore on. She walked down Alex's stairs on her own so he wouldn't see her limping but did catch the concern flashing over Ahmed's face when she'd gritted her teeth in pain walking to the car. The damn thing hurt like a bitch, but it was the Wimbledon Round of 16, she was about to be announced to the Court 1 crowd. Withdrawing simply wasn't an option.

"Game plan," Dom said from the corner of the trainer's room. He was clearly done arguing with her about it, but she almost wished he'd bring it up. If he asked her right now whether she wanted to play, she wasn't sure what her answer would be. As that thought settled in her head, she felt her stomach twist.

She'd never withdrawn before, not for anything. She didn't think she had it in her to just give up without even trying, but this pain, this was something she'd never felt before and it was really, really scary. She must have torn it worse, playing on it the way she had sooner than the doctors had suggested. But the pain had subsided long enough to trick her into thinking the worst was behind her, and this was the most important tournament of her life. Now, she didn't know if she'd done the right thing. In fact, she was pretty sure she'd been wrong all along. Dom and the trainers and Alex and everyone else had been right. Her ankle throbbed again; apparently, it wanted to be included in there as well. It had tried to tell her. It had swelled and twinged, but she'd kept on playing anyway. What had Alex called her? A stubborn mule. That was her, a total ass.

"Keep her moving, vary up my serves and serve and volley, especially on her second serve."

"Good," he said. "You don't have any new shots to tell me about, things you've been working on with Alex without informing me?"

Penny snorted. The miraculous appearance of Jasmine's one-handed backhand was still rankling their coach days after she'd debuted it in the junior tournament.

"No surprises, I promise."

"Good. I'll see you out there."

Her coach left, but just as he made it through the door, another familiar face peaked in. "Hello, mind if I join you for a bit?" Anna Russell said, slipping into the room after nodding a goodbye to Dom.

"Sure."

"I just sent Alex off to his match, so I thought I'd come in and say good luck to you before yours."

Penny stood up to give Alex's mom a hug, but as she did, the pain shot up her leg and her entire body buckled. She blinked and a lump formed in her throat. It choked her for a moment and her eyes watered.

"Oh, sweetheart, what's the matter?" Anna asked, rushing forward and taking Penny's hands in hers, squeezing lightly. "Are you okay?"

Inhaling a shaky breath and letting the tears fall, she shook her head. "No, I don't think I am."

"What do you need? What can I do?"

"Nothing. You can't do anything." Penny felt something inside of her break. "I have to withdraw."

~

The trip to the hospital was a quiet one. Instead of an ambulance, Penny insisted that their driver Ahmed bring her and so she sat at the back of the car while her phone blew up, blinging over and over again in her hand until she just couldn't stand it anymore and she turned the damn thing off. Across the car, Anna Russell sat, her face carefully blank.

"Thank you for coming with me," she whispered, even though she was facing the window, staring unseeingly out onto the London streets.

"Of course, sweetheart. Alex would want me here with you when he couldn't be."

Penny glanced back at her and tried to smile, but it was impossible.

She was hustled into the actual hospital to avoid any cameras spotting her, but the paparazzi were all still back at Wimbledon, watching the actual matches. There was a back up for scans and Dom showed up, slamming his way through the doors and rushing over to them, breathing heavily as if he'd run all the way from Wimbledon.

"Dom," Penny said, but that damn lump reappeared, stopping her words. He had other places to be. Alex was playing right now on Centre Court; Indy and Jasmine were about to go head to head in the junior tournament. He didn't need to sit here with her, waiting for a doctor to take a picture of her ankle and tell her what she already knew. She was hurt, maybe worse than she'd ever been in her life and it was all her fault.

"No arguing, okay?" Dom took a seat on her other side, sending a nod to Anna and out of the corner of her eye, Penny caught him mouthing, "thank you." Her coach took her hand in his and squeeze. "You're gonna be okay, Pen. I promise. Whatever it is. You're going to be okay."

"Miss Harrison," a nurse called out after what felt like an eternity. A middle-aged, slight-looking woman with light blonde hair approached and moved behind the wheelchair Penny had been positioned in when she arrived. "Let's go take a look at that ankle, young lady."

The MRI machine was an older model, quite loud and anyone who suffered from claustrophobia would have lost their mind as the machine moaned and groaned it's way to a scan. When she'd had her scans done in France, the hospital had used a new 3-D imaging scanner that had created an amazing computer image of her ankle, but the MRI was good enough to show the doctor everything he needed to know.

"You tore your posterior talofibular ligament."

"That's the same one I hurt in France."

"Yes," the Doctor agreed. "It started as a very tiny tear. You played on that ankle too soon, Penelope."

She nodded. "I know."

"See that it doesn't happen again. Six to eight weeks. Minimum."

That stupid lump was back and she nodded, but her mind was whirring. Six to eight weeks. The beginning of August. Most of the summer would be completely lost and it would leave her with three weeks to prep for the US Open.

"Penny, are you listening to what the doctor is saying?" Dom asked, knowing that she wasn't.

"Yes, sorry. Six to eight weeks. Stay off it. Rest. No playing on it too soon."

"Next time, you might not be so lucky, Penelope," the doctor said, gathering up the files and handing them over to her. "I'll be available to consult with your doctor back in the States if you need."

"Thank you, Doctor," Dom said, reaching over the desk to shake his hand.

"Yes, thank you," Penny said, standing on her brand new air cast and adjusting the crutches under her arms, not quite believing that she'd just thanked someone for telling her she couldn't play for nearly two months.

"Do you want to go home? I can get you a car."

"No, I want to go back. Alex is still playing, right?"

~

He wasn't just *still playing*. He was locked in a five-set marathon with his third-round opponent, an American veteran, Frank Masters, a player they all knew well. Masters was on the downside of a decade-long career on tour, but that didn't mean he still didn't have a lot of game left in him.

"Game, Mr. Russell," the chair umpire said just as Penny slid into her seat in the player's box on Centre Court. She could feel the cameras turning and zooming in as both Alex and Frank headed for their chairs and the TV stations went to commercial break. The crowd murmured around her and Alex's eyes were drawn to them. Someone must have told him what happened. Penny just slid the necklace she always wore out of her shirt and held in it in her hand, lifting it for him to see. His mouth was tight and he didn't smile but simply nodded and then she saw his eyes glaze over as he slipped back into competition mode, focusing on what he had to do to finish out the match.

"He'll be fine," Anna said from beside her. "He knows how to turn off the world out there, almost as well as you do."

"Yeah, I know," Penny said, sitting back in her seat.

"He told me he'd given you that," she said, nodding towards Penny's clenched fist.

"It's the best present I've ever gotten."

Anna nodded. "I hope you don't mind, sweetheart, but I took the liberty of calling your parents while we were at the hospital."

"No, it's okay. Saves me the trouble of having to do it."

"You should call them anyway."

"Oh, I will, I just…they're going to be upset and I don't really want to hear how sorry people are yet. They shouldn't be sorry. I was an idiot and now I'm paying the price."

"You're not an idiot. You are a fierce competitor and sometimes that makes you blind to certain things, but you're not an idiot. I've never seen anyone want it the way you do, Penny. Not even Alex. I remember the first time he laid eyes on you."

"What?"

"Oh, he didn't tell you about that? It was around this time last year."

Penny's thoughts flew back to a night back home when he'd confessed to seeing her for the first time and wanting her even then, but he hadn't been specific. "He mentioned something, but…"

"You were on a practice court and he was up next and completely surrounded by people wanting his autograph, mostly young women, daughters of club members, some of the wives as well." She paused, her eyebrows wiggling and

Penny laughed. "Anyway, finally, security came and broke it up a bit and he turned around as you were coming off the court with Dom. Dom stopped and said hello to us, but you were in your own little world, sweetheart. Still had your racket in your hand, mumbling to yourself, something about staying low and driving through the ball and Alex asked Dom who you were. He told him your name and I knew it, right then, that it was over. You should have seen him in that practice session. Completely distracted. Couldn't hit, how do they say it where you're from? The broad side of a barn? It would have been hilarious if he didn't have a quarterfinal match that night."

"He won that night," Penny said, her eyes glued to the man on the court.

"He did because he has what you have, that need to be the best and the fight to just put everything else away and *win*."

"Well, I won't be doing any of that for a while now," she said, lifting her leg, still feeling it sting a little bit, even with that smallest of motions.

"Sure you will. Every day you stay off it, it's healing. That's a win. Every day you listen to Dom and the trainers, that's a win. Every day you get closer to getting back on the court and winning the U.S. Open, that's a win too."

"The Open…" she trailed off.

"Don't pretend like you weren't thinking about that as soon as you got the news."

"How did you…"

"Because I was with Alex when the doctors told him six to eight weeks after his knee injury in Australia, because as soon he could train again, he called up Dom and got on a flight across the Atlantic Ocean to get back to where he was before. So that's what you have to do, Penny. Go back home. Rest. Recover. Then kick some ass in New York."

"Time," the chair umpire said, calling the players back to the court for the next game.

"New York."

Anna patted her hand lightly. "Indeed."

Chapter 22

June 28th

Indy slept late. Really late. Late enough that the whole house was empty by the time she slid out of bed. She wandered down to the kitchen, knowing she'd have to get her butt in gear soon and get ready. She and Jasmine were set to play in the Girls Junior quarterfinals, in just a few hours. She'd been at her match the day before and she'd been just as shocked as everyone else to see Jasmine wipe the floor with Adelaide Brennan with a shiny new backhand and a confidence radiating off of her that

Indy hadn't seen in her former doubles partner since the OBX Classic, months ago.

Just as she grabbed a banana from the bowl at the center of the island, she heard the chime of the doorbell. A quick glance through the peephole and she rolled her eyes.

"Are you still my agent?" she asked, throwing open the door. Caroline Morneau stood on the other side of the threshold, perfectly put together as usual in a sleek white pencil skirt and white lace top, perfect for a day at Wimbledon.

"Of course I'm still your agent, Indiana," she said, not waiting for an invitation inside and simply striding through the door.

"What's up, Caroline?" she asked, following the other woman into the library and peeling her banana.

She took a large envelope from her tan brief case and unsealed it, pulling out a packet of paper and handing it to Indy. "This was just sent to me from Adidas."

"Adidas?" Indy said, flipping through the pages. It was mostly legalese and so she looked back up at Caroline.

"A complete outfitting deal for the rest of the season. And next year, you will get a chance to design your own tournament line."

"What about what you said before? About Jasmine and them wanting us to sign together?"

Caroline waved a hand in the air, dismissing it. "The point is moot now. After your little outburst the other day, you're no longer the tall, blonde bombshell ready to explode onto the scene. Now you're a risk and for now, we will simply take what is offered to us and be grateful."

"I'm not a…"

"You are, Indiana. The sponsors don't know what to expect from you, they don't know who will be taking the court, the girl who blew through the competition at the French Open Juniors or the girl who couldn't keep it together long enough to utter a 'no comment.' It is bad business to make potential sponsors question your mental strength."

Indy opened her mouth to argue again, but then she let it go. "So this is the best deal we'll be able to get now?"

"It is easily the best offer we have received and I believe you should sign it. Your father has already looked it over and given his okay. You'll see his signature at the bottom of the page."

"Yeah, only a few more months of that," Indy said, still flipping through the pages, not seeing the words at all, but wanting something to do with her hands. This was it. She was going to be sponsored by Adidas. "Okay, do you have a pen?"

"As it happens," Caroline said, holding one out to her.

She scrawled her name just below her father's and sighed. It was done.

"You've made an excellent decision, Indiana. They'll be in touch after the tournament in regards to any commitments and I'd expect a rather large shipment of gear by the time you arrive home." Caroline took the papers back from her, slipping them back into the envelope and then into her briefcase. "I will see you later at the match. Good luck, chérie."

Indy walked her out and as she opened the door, they saw Jack getting out of one of the tournament cars.

"Ah, perfect." Caroline said, her heels click-clacking down the stone steps to the car and speaking to the driver.

"Hey, what are you doing back here?" Indy asked as Jack leaned down to kiss her cheek. "Forget it, I don't care." He was one of the only people she wanted to celebrate with. She wound her arms around his broad shoulders and used them as leverage to leap into his arms. He caught her under her thighs and as was their habit, backed her into the wall of the foyer. Her back hit the solid surface and she groaned as he lifted his mouth to hers and nipped at her lower lip. She tightened her legs around him and he echoed the noise she'd just made. She felt the reverberations through his chest and into her own body.

"Wait, wait," he said, breaking the kiss and sucking a breath of air into his lungs. He moved off the wall and guided her back down to the floor. "As much as I'd like to take advantage of the empty house, I wanted to talk to you about something before you saw the press release. I didn't get a chance to tell you before now because the papers weren't signed and I don't make it a practice to talk about business until everything is official, but she signed this morning, so…"

Her mind was still spinning from the way he'd just pulled away. "Wait, who signed what?"

"Jasmine. I signed her on as a client."

Indy let the words turn over in her head. Jack had signed Jasmine. He was her agent. "That's…that's great. Congratulations," she managed to say, still a little in shock. Now Caroline's dismissal of her question earlier made sense. The reason Adidas had offered her a deal worth signing was because Jasmine had forgone her amateur status. She was a pro and now they'd be able to sign them both. She really hadn't given much thought to the idea that the only reason she'd be offered a sponsorship was because her doubles partner—or really her former doubles partner—was able to sign as well. It meant that they didn't just want her for her talent, for what she could offer them, but the package deal that came with being one half of Randazzo and Gaffney. She tried to take a deep breath, but her chest was heavy and tight. She forced herself to focus on Jack, who wasn't done talking.

"I'm so glad you're not upset. I know things have been a little rocky between you two since you had to drop doubles, but she approached me about it and after that performance she put on yesterday I couldn't tell her no." Jack leaned in to peck her lightly on the lips.

"Of course not. You had to sign her. Jasmine's going to be a great player and you're going to be amazing for her."

"Yeah, I think it's going to be a good partnership. Her parents were less than thrilled. They'd been pushing for her to try out NCAA, but she wants what she wants. I've already heard from Nike, Adidas and Lacoste."

"Adidas?" Indy asked. "Not surprising."

"Why?"

"Because I just signed a contract with them like thirty seconds ago."

"You're kidding? Indiana, that's amazing," he said, stepping up to her and pulling her into his arms. He spun around and she had to wind her arms around his shoulders to stay with him. Lowering her to her feet, he leaned in and kissed her. "Congratulations."

"Do you want to hear about the deal?"

"Outfitting?" he asked, quirking an eyebrow.

"You *knew!*" she accused, poking him in the chest.

Jack laughed, grabbing her hand and rubbing the spot she'd injured. "Word gets around, but I have another surprise for you?"

"Yeah? What's that?"

He reached down into his briefcase and handed her a thick envelope. "It was sent to OBX, but I had Roy keeping an eye out for it."

She slid her hand under the seal and pulled a piece of thick parchment paper out. Her diploma. All that hard work she'd put in and she'd done it. And now, even if it wasn't quite what they'd hoped for, she had a solid sponsorship deal with Adidas. She was a professional tennis player. It was everything she and her mom had ever dreamed of together and it was *real*. Now all that was left was to show everyone that she wasn't a risk; that she could go out on the big stage and *win*—her stomach twisted—if she could keep the damn nerves under control.

"Go on, get dressed. You've got a match today."

"Right, yeah, a match," she said, mindlessly leaning up to kiss him and then wandering back upstairs. She felt her stomach turn again and tried to keep it at bay, gripping the paper between her fingers, feeling it bend under the pressure. Not again.

~

"Indy," Dom said, tapping her shaking leg. "You in there?"

"Yeah, sorry," she said, looking up at her coach. They were in the player's lounge and Jasmine was sitting just a few tables away, also waiting for the call to go out to the court. "Game plan. Don't get into long rallies, first serves and don't get cute."

"Good," he said. "Play tough, play smart."

"I got it, Dom," she said, plastering a smile across her face and nodding in Jasmine's direction. "Go ahead."

As he walked away, her stomach twisted again and then her eyes widened as bile started to rise in her throat. Her eyes flashed around the room and she held her breath and then swallowed down whatever was attempting to come up. She needed to calm down. How did she used to do it? Calm down whenever she felt like this? Glancing across the room, she saw Dom talking to Jasmine and she remembered. Jasmine had calmed her down. Their partnership, going out onto the court together, and now? Now that was gone and it hit her like a ton of bricks. The bile rose again and she pushed herself out of the chair, sprinting for the bathroom. She was so screwed.

~

There was a huge crowd, even more people than had shown up at Court 1 for her match against Penny in the main draw, and the tournament had anticipated it, scheduling the match at Court 17, which held more spectators than the normal junior match would draw. What she wouldn't give now for that out-of-the-way court she'd played her first-round match on, just a chain link fence and only enough room for a couple of dozen people in the stands.

Indy's stomach rolled, but thankfully, there was nothing left to come up. She could practically see herself back at OBX facing Jasmine. She'd come out on top in that match, but that was mostly because Jasmine had tightened up and Indy had been able to forget the nerves, anger replacing any fear she'd had on the court. She couldn't count on the anger now. If anything, Jasmine had reason to be angry with her, not the other way around.

She barely remembered warm-ups, just going through the motions; she could feel Jasmine's eyes on her the entire time, probing, questioning, probably wondering what the hell was wrong with her. She'd know in a minute.

"Players to the center of the court," the chair umpire said, waving both of them to the net. Indy waited and took a deep steadying breath before standing from her chair and walking to the net.

"Miss Gaffney, call it in the air," the umpire said.

"Tails," she said, and the coin landed on the green grass of the Wimbledon court. Though it was wearing in patches from use throughout the week, at the net, it was still pristine.

He bent over to grab the coin. "It is tails," he declared. "Miss Gaffney."

Her mouth opened, but no sound came out and she hesitated. She should serve. That was her bread and butter.

"Miss Gaffney."

"Sorry, yeah, I'll serve." She looked up to the players box and everyone was there. Teddy, Penny, Alex, Paolo and that Natalie girl who was playing doubles with Jasmine, bouncing in her seat and snapping pictures with her phone. Just behind them sat Dom, Jack, Caroline and apparently, Mr. and Mrs. Randazzo had decided to take a flight in. And in a moment where she was sure her own subconscious was just screwing with her, she wished her dad had decided to just show up, like he had in France.

The ball boy offered her a few options and she chose two at random, tucking one underneath her skirt, the other she bounced beneath her racket face, getting the feel of the court.

"Play," the umpire called and at his words, her stomach did yet another somersault. There was no way to calm down, so she just had to play with it and however this was going to turn out, she'd have to live with it.

Taking a deep breath, she reared back and fired a serve down the center of the court as hard as she possibly could. It felt good, getting some tension out of her body.

"Out!" the line judge called, raising an arm to indicate that it had landed in the opposite service box.

She pulled the second ball out from the hidden pocket in her skirt and sent another screaming liner toward the general direction of the middle of the court.

"Out," the judge yelled again, the same arm rising.

"Love – 15."

"Okay, easy back on the throttle, Indy," she muttered to herself, taking up another ball. Except if she did that, she took away her best weapon. She needed to get that power serve in. It was the only way she was going to win this match. Jasmine would run her all over the court if she just played to get her serves in. She'd get bogged down in long points and with that new backhand of hers, there wouldn't be anything Indy could do about it.

She was so screwed.

Chapter 23

June 28th

"Game, Miss Randazzo. Miss Randazzo leads the second set, five games to two."

Jasmine pumped her fist and pointed to the ball boy, who was also holding onto her towel. The day had started out pleasant, but the late afternoon sun had burned off all the cloud cover and it was pounding down on the court. She'd worked up a fine sheen of sweat, but it was nothing like the heat they trained in back home. At the thought of home, her eyes traveled to the box in the corner of the court where her parents were sitting.

Dom had texted her early that morning, her phone vibrating on her nightstand. The message had been simple, that there was a surprise for her downstairs. She figured maybe he'd sent her some new rackets or that maybe her parents had sent good luck flowers. But as she'd descended the stairs, she'd caught sight of them standing in the foyer and had flown down the rest of the stairs, letting out a high-pitched shriek as she launched herself into her dad's arms. Just a month ago in Paris, she hadn't wanted her parents there. She was afraid she would embarrass them with her performance, but now, she was flying high. She knew she could win and she wanted them there to see it. She thought Dom had been the one to invite them, but when she asked, her dad's eyes had flickered across the room to where Teddy sat. He nodded and then quickly excused himself to go see Penny's match. She'd just managed to utter a thank you to his retreating back, completely bewildered by the gesture, but then her mom had swept her up into a hug. Teddy was in the box today, sitting just behind her parents and apparently this was his peace offering. It was a pretty damn good one and when the match was over, she was going to thank him properly.

Her eyes moved from him, down the row to the man who'd been the source of conflict between her and her best friend. Paolo's eyes were on her. She could feel that steely blue gaze following her all over the court and it sent a wave of comfort over her. He'd kept silent for most of the match, so had the rest of the people in the box, a nod of respect to both her and Indy. But she knew that he was cheering her on, knew that he was behind her all the way. Now, she just had to finish it.

"Time," the chair umpire said and she stood, grabbing her racket and her towel and tossing it to the ball boy again. One more game and this match would be hers and there would only be a couple of matches standing between her and the Wimbledon Junior Championship. But one match at a time. She'd gotten cocky the last time she and Indy had played, had thought victory was fait accompli. Jasmine wasn't going to make that same mistake twice. Four more points and then she could celebrate.

It was Indy's serve and after a disastrous first set, the girl who had one of the fiercest serves in the world had backed off considerably just to get the ball in play. She knew Indy hadn't *wanted* to do it, but after dropping her first two games on serve, it had been necessary, though too late to salvage the set. Ever since, Jasmine took full advantage of knowing that anything Indy sent her way would be more than manageable to return.

"Play," the chair umpire declared and Indy didn't hesitate, placing a nice, safe serve in the center of the box. Jasmine stepped into it and fired a forehand cross-court. Indy managed to block it back and they both retreated to the baseline, sending groundstroke after groundstroke over the net. Then Indy made the mistake of going to Jasmine's backhand side and she swiveled her hips, unleashing her new one-handed backhand over the net and down the line, a shot that would have been impossible for her just a week earlier.

"Love – 15."

The crowd cheered and for the first time all match, Jasmine actually noticed how many people were there watching them. They were one of the later day session matches and the main courts had cleared out already so the stands were completely full. Somehow, a junior girls' match had become the most interesting battle on the Wimbledon grounds.

After a quick wipe of the towel over her face, she returned to the baseline and waited for Indy to gather herself on the other side of the court. The tall blonde was taking her time, using the towel on her face, arms and legs, then finally taking the ball girl's offerings and tossing a few of the options back. Delaying the inevitable.

Finally, Indy approached the baseline and Jasmine set herself, bent over at the waist, her racket out in front, weight on the balls of her feet. Indy coiled her body down toward the ground and then exploded through the ball, taking a chance that Jasmine wouldn't be prepared for it. She was. Her return was even faster than the serve that preceded it, burying it deep into the corner before Indy could even take a step in that direction.

"Love – 30."

"Come on!" Jasmine yelled, pumping her fist and the crowd roared back at her. It had been a hell of a shot.

Two more. Two more points and she'd have this.

"Quiet please," the chair umpire asked the fans and they settled into a low buzz.

Indy was ready faster this time, bouncing on her feet, her usual serve routine and Jasmine stood at the baseline, ready for anything. The serve came hard and fast again, but long.

"Out."

They reset and Jasmine bounced up in perfect position as another laser beam fired across the court. She fired a return and it landed long, but the judge on her side of the court had already called, "Out!"

Double fault.

"Love – 40."

Her chest tightened and so she inhaled slowly through her nose, trying to block out noise on the court. The crowd was fired up and applauding, but Jasmine studied the strings of her racket, pushing them back into straight lines that had become a little funky dealing with the velocity of Indy's serve. The next point had to be just another point, just like the first point of the match, no more, no less. Another deep breath and she moved to the baseline.

The next seconds were a blur. A serve wide and high came over the net and she just reacted with her backhand, slicing it back over the court and then the words, "Game. Set. Match, 6-2, 6-2, Miss Randazzo."

Then nothing, just a haze of shaking Indy's hand, then the chair umpire's and heading out to the center of the court to applaud the crowd who applauded her right back. She'd blown a kiss toward the box and she'd watched as her parents thought it was to them for a moment, before Paolo lifted his own hand to his lips and blew one right back. Her dad's face had been priceless.

Now she was back in the locker room, accepting congratulations from other players, most of who were arriving for the night session but had caught the match on the closed circuit TV in the locker room and player's lounge. She pulled the draw from her racket bag and took a look at her potential opponents, recognizing the names almost immediately, both were girls she'd faced before and both were girls she'd beaten. Her breath caught in her throat. She could win this whole thing. In just a couple more days, she could be the Wimbledon Junior Champion and with the way she and Natalie were playing in doubles, maybe she could take home two trophies.

"Hey," a voice called from the end of the row and Jasmine looked up, folding the paper neatly and placing it back in her bag.

"Hey," she said back, turning to see Indy walking toward her, showered and dressed. Jasmine shook her head. "What the hell happened to you out there?"

Indy sat down on the bench opposite her and shrugged. "Got nervous."

"Clearly. I thought you'd figured that out."

"Yeah me too. Listen," Indy said. "I just wanted to say that I'm sorry."

Jasmine shook her head. "You did what you felt was right."

"Never thought being a pro would make me a shitty friend."

"It's part of the job," Jasmine said. "Did Jack tell you?"

"He did. It's awesome news. He's going to do big things for you."

"He's really good at his job. I heard you signed with Adidas."

"News travels fast."

"That's a really big deal, Indy."

"I know, sort of part of what got me nervous."

"You gotta stop doing that. When we get home, we'll get you to a sports psychologist or something."

"Great, a shrink. I can tell him all about my issues."

Jasmine reached out and hesitated for a second before squeezing Indy's shoulder. "You can leave me out of it."

Indy's brow furrowed.

"No, I mean, we're cool. I'm not one of your issues, unless that beating you just took scarred you for life."

Indy snorted. "Ouch, Jas. Too soon."

Jasmine giggled. "Sorry."

"No, you're not," Indy said, "but I guess I deserved it."

"Maybe a little."

"Are you two done yet?" a new voice joined in, followed by the click of metal hitting the ground. Penny was swinging herself between her crutches, her foot in an air cast. "There are a lot of people out there who want to congratulate you." She nodded to Indy, "and console you."

"Maybe we should just stay in here for a little while," Indy said. "Come on, Pen, take a load off." She patted the empty spot on the bench beside her.

"That's all I'm going to be doing for a while," Penny said, lowering herself to the wooden seat and leaning her crutches next to her. "No tennis for me."

"Sucks," Jasmine and Indy said at the same time.

"It does, but that means I get to live the hard-court season vicariously through you guys and then New York."

"New York," Indy said, the side of her mouth quirking up.

"Hang on guys, I still have a tournament to win."

"Please, didn't you look at the draw?" Indy asked. "You've got this. This match today, this was the championship."

Penny smiled and bumped Indy's shoulder. "Enjoy it while you can. You're both gonna get wildcards to the Open and by then, I'll be as good as new."

"Yay, I can't wait to lose like that *again*," Indy drawled and Jasmine rolled her eyes.

"Let's go guys, enough. I just won a pretty big match and I think my Dad is probably interrogating Paolo as we speak."

"Yeah Paolo, when did that happen?" Indy asked as she helped Penny stand, "because damn girl, you owe me one."

"What am I missing?" Penny asked and Jasmine felt her cheeks get hot as they started out of the locker room.

"It was back in Paris..." Indy said and Jasmine let the words wash over her, Indy making it sound like she'd thrown Jasmine into Paolo's arms, Penny laughing at all the right parts. She followed them out of the locker room, taking in the sea of faces smiling at them and she smiled back, trying to memorize the feeling because, for right now, everything was absolutely perfect.

ACKNOWLEDGEMENTS

Writing my first book was hard. Writing my second book felt utterly impossible. There were dozens of people who helped get this book out into the world.

First, Michelle Wolfson, my fantastic agent, because without you none of this would have happened.

Megan McKeever for your seemingly unending patience and guidance in getting this book where it needed to go.

Lisa, Waynn, Jennifer and the entire team at Coliloquy for believing in me and then sticking with me!

To Anna Kovatcheva. I didn't think I could love a cover more than I loved GSM's. I was wrong. This one was perfect!

My new team at Vook: Alexis, Koa and Allison. You all just stepped in and just made this work.

My faithful OBXers who kept me going with emails and tweets asking when this book was coming! Guys, it's FINALLY here!

And last, but never least, my amazing family because without your support I never would have dreamed I could write one book, let alone two!

ABOUT THE AUTHOR

Jennifer Iacopelli was born in New York and has no plans to leave...ever. Growing up, she read everything she could get her hands on, but her favorite authors were Laura Ingalls Wilder, L.M. Montgomery and Frances Hodgson Burnett all of whom wrote about kick-ass girls before it was cool for girls to be kick-ass. She earned a Bachelor's degree in Adolescence Education and English Literature quickly followed up by a Master's in Library Science, which lets her frolic all day with her books and computers, leaving plenty of time in the evenings to write and yell at the Yankees, Giants and her favorite tennis players through the TV.

Follow her on twitter @jennifercarolyn or on her website www.jenniferiacopelli.com